Holy B

CW00859893

Norma Curtis

StarLit

First published in 2013 as an eBook original. This version 2014

ISBN-13:978-1493579525
ISBN-10:1493579525

Front cover design: Kai Collier-Thomas
kaiser23@hotmail.co.uk

End cover designed by Joe Curtis
joeacurtis@gmail.com

For Paul and Joe, with love

Acknowledgements

Tal's triads are taken from Trioedd Ynys Prydein, edited by Rachel Bromwich and published by the University of Wales Press. My thanks to the University of Wales Press and the National Library of Wales for permitting me to use some of the triads in this book.

Table of Contents

Chapter One

'Do you want to hear a secret?'

The old man came to life from the shadows of his chair, making me jump.

As I turned to look at him he smiled with delight and adjusted his black tie carefully as if he was ready to do business.

I'd come to the care home to look for Nain. The day room was gloomy. Red velvet curtains shut out the sun and white-haired ladies dozed quietly, heads nodding. The brightest thing in the room was the plasma television tuned in to Comedy Central.

The second brightest thing was the old man.

'Well?' he asked eagerly.

Did I want to hear a secret? 'Depends,' I said. 'What's it about?'

He bent forward and rested his elbows on his bony knees. 'It's about a severed head.'

1

I wasn't expecting that. 'No thanks,' I said, 'I'm squeamish about that sort of thing.'

He raised his bushy eyebrows in surprise. 'Squeamish about holy bones? But it's a perfect Head!' he protested. 'An extraordinary Head! And after it was cut off, it was no less beautiful than when it was attached!' His eyes sparkled. 'It has incredible powers, too,' he added softly.

He was crazy, but it costs nothing to be kind according to Nain, so I asked, 'What kind of powers?'

'The power to protect the country.'

'Oh.' Obviously that's a good thing, but it wasn't actually useful to me personally. I was just about to say so when he smiled gently, as though he knew my thoughts.

'It can give you anything that you've ever dreamed about.'

Okay. Now I was interested.

Basically I dreamed about getting rich, winning gold at the next Olympics and passing my exams without revising. But my biggest, longest-lasting, most hopeful dream was that I'd see my mother again. She's been gone for four years now, long story, and when she phones she doesn't mention coming home any more. If I had this severed head, that's the dream I'd use it for. 'It sounds great,' I said cheerfully. 'I'll give it a go. Where is it?'

The old man rubbed his palm against his jaw and all the happiness faded out of him. He slumped slowly back in his chair and his black jacket rose up around his neck as if he'd suddenly shrunk a size or two. 'That's the problem,' he said. 'I don't remember.'

'What?' I had the feeling that I'd just got all excited over nothing but I stayed cool. 'Take your time – where did you have it last?' That's something my dad always says when I lose stuff. Trust me, it doesn't help.

'I don't know,' the old man said sadly. 'I've lost my memories, you see?'

'Yes,' I replied, feeling sorry for myself for getting hopeful. But I was sorry for him, too. He had his own dreams - he probably imagined going somewhere adventurous in his suit and tie instead of sitting there all day watching television in the dark.

Suddenly Nain was calling to me from the other end of the room, waving wildly.

'Ava Jones!' she yelled, waking up the old lady next her. 'Ava! Over here!'

'I'd better go,' I told the old man, 'before she shouts the place down. If you remember where the Head is, let me know. I'm going to be here every day for a while, okay?'

He nodded, and then he closed his eyes and shut me out.

I hurried over to Nain. Her white hair and her white bandages glowed in the dark.

There were a lot of things I wanted to ask her – things I'd waited a whole day to find out.

chapter Two

Since my Mum left home I've spent the
school holidays with my Nain in Wales
because my dad only gets two weeks off
and he doesn't trust me at home by myself.

Nain is pronounced *nine* and it's Welsh
for grandmother. We have a good time
together. She's bossy but kind and she lets
me choose the food we eat, which means
No Salads. There's a leisure centre near
her house with a great pool in it as well as
the River Dee and the Blue Lagoon to
swim in. I love swimming. I'm not skinny,
for a start, which is good. Fat floats. Drop
some butter into a sink full of water and
see. Trust me, you can try this at home.

BUT – yesterday evening the phone
rang and everything changed.

I was lying on the red rug watching The
X Factor and Caroline, my dad's
girlfriend, was doing her toenails on the
red sofa, so Dad answered it. Suddenly he
said 'What?' and his voice was loud and

sharp over the television. Caroline looked at him and picked up the remote to mute the tv.

'Yes, I'm her son,' Dad said.

The room seemed to get cold. I sat up, cross-legged, and looked at him. For a long time he didn't speak; he just listened, nodding his head now and then and rubbing his ginger hair. It was obvious that something bad had happened.

While I was worrying, Dad put the phone down. 'Nain's been found heading towards Rhos mountain in her nightdress,' he said, and his face was tight and pale.

I was really shocked. 'In her nightdress?' It was hard to believe, because Nain never leaves the house without a coat and umbrella. 'But why would she do that?'

He shrugged. 'She wasn't wearing shoes so she's hurt her feet.'

'No shoes?' She didn't even go barefoot around the house!

Caroline screwed the cap on the nail polish and put it down on the arm of the sofa. 'You're worrying about shoes?' she said to me, wiggling her toes to dry them.

6

'The woman took off in her nightclothes, that's the point, right, Michael?'

Dad didn't look at her.

'Let's face it,' she went on calmly, 'we all saw this coming.'

I hadn't. It was true that Nain had become a bit forgetful. She would ring up on a Sunday and ask me why I wasn't in school, and in shops she would put the money on the counter and let the sales person count it instead of doing it for herself. But that wasn't in the same league as heading for the mountains in her sleepwear, barefoot.

Dad looked as though he didn't know what to say. I stood up quickly and hugged him and said she would be all right. When he didn't reply, I got worried. 'She will be all right, won't she?'

'I don't know.' He lowered his head and butted me gently so that we were nose-to-nose. 'It sounds as if she can't look after herself anymore.'

'So? She can come and live with us.'

Caroline made a funny snort in the back of her nose. 'What?' she said when we looked at her. 'She's got dementia!'

'What's dementia? Is it curable?'

Dad didn't answer. 'I'm going to drive up there right now,' he said, straightening up. He went to the fish tank, and dropped in some flakes. The goldfish swam out of the ornamental skull's eyes to eat them, their lips making ripples on the water. 'You don't have to come, Caroline.'

'I'm coming,' I said quickly. I was going anyway; I'd already packed. I headed upstairs to get my bag. It was different for Caroline – she'd only known Nain for two years, since she and Dad met, whereas Dad and I had known her all our lives.

While Dad got ready, I rang Rosie, my best friend. I sat on my bed and told her the whole story.

'She was in her nightdress?' Rosie asked. 'That's so embarrassing!'

'I know!'

'Was she sleepwalking?'

I hadn't thought of that. 'Maybe,' I said.

'Sleepwalking's dangerous, because if someone's sleepwalking and you wake them up suddenly, they die.'

I shivered at the thought.

'And who found her? Was it the mountain rescue guys?'

'Probably.' Talking to Rosie it was obvious there was a lot we didn't know, like how long she'd been walking for and how far up the mountain she'd got. 'I'll let you know as soon as I find out. Okay. I have to go,' I said, because even though I was ready I felt as if I had to do everything at top speed.

Half an hour later we were in the car, driving to Wales.

The drive takes three and a half hours, and I looked through the window and listened to my iPod and somewhere after the M1 I had an argument with Caroline and then I fell asleep.

Caroline's okay, most of the time. I told my dad 'No Steps' after he and my mum divorced, so he didn't bring her home for ages. Then I started wondering what she was like, and finally I asked to meet her, just so that I knew who I was hating.

Caroline is slim. That's because she doesn't eat.

She is tall, with blonde hair like mine and she lives on coffee, wine and nicotine chewing gum. When we go out, people say, 'And is this your sister?' Caroline and

I fold our arms and roll our eyes at each other when they say that.

When we first met, I did hate her.

She hated me, too. She out-hates me in most things. She hates most people, dogs, cats, all fish including our goldfish, pillows that are not goose-down, and getting wet. She has another list of things she loathes, like: cheap make-up, leather jeans, soaps, cockroaches, karaoke, and untidiness.

That first time Dad brought her home to meet me, she came into the lounge wearing a red suit and high heels and she frowned at me. 'Well?'

'Well what?'

'You've met me. Are you happy now?'

Dad was grinning proudly behind her.

'No,' I said. I thought of something my friends had mentioned when they'd gone through the same thing. 'Did you bring me a gift?'

She opened her handbag and started taking things out. 'Car keys – you want my car? My wallet? My lipstick? My house keys? What? What do you want?'

I stared at her. She was completely mad.

' - packet of TicTacs?' She took them out of the bag and rattled them at me.

I imagined suddenly owning her car and her house and I wanted to laugh, but I didn't. 'Have you got any money?' I asked hopefully.

This set her off again. 'How much? Ten? Twenty? Fifty? Here. Take it. Have it all.' She snatched a bundle of cash out of her wallet and pushed it at me.

It looked more than it was because in amongst it were receipts and dry cleaning tickets and things, but I took it and she closed her bag with a snap.

'I'm glad that's over,' she said, flicking her hair away from her face.

'Me too.'

She turned to Dad. 'Get us two black coffees, Michael. I'm a Celebrity's on. I hate it. Especially Ant and Dec.'

I hated it too, so we watched it together.

By the time I woke up we had arrived in Nain's village and it was dark.

'Where is everyone?' Caroline asked as she got out of the car, looking along the deserted street. 'Where are all the people?'

'They're either at home or in the pub,' I said, putting my iPod in my bag. 'Or in the bus shelter.' That's where the boys hung out. It was made of brick, and it had a roof and a red plastic seat.

'In the bus shelter? What can you do in a bus shelter?'

Sometimes I didn't know how Caroline had got to thirty-seven without learning anything at all about life. 'You can hang out.'

We went into Nain's house. In all my life I'd never been there without her, and I was afraid I would miss her so much I'd feel ill.

But the house was full of her and it cheered me up. It smelled nice, and her antique furniture was shiny and smooth, and the photographs were happy and her ornaments were neatly arranged. I walked around looking at her things, and Dad put the kettle on.

I followed him into the kitchen and saw some brown marks on the tiles. 'Dad, you should have taken your shoes off,' I told him, pointing. 'Look what you've done!'

He lifted his foot up to look. 'They're clean.' He looked at the marks. 'Oh, it's mud,' he said. 'Get out before you spread it around everywhere. Quick!'

'Hey, that's not mud – '

'Quick!' He flicked a dishcloth at me and pushed me out of the door and turned the key.

'I know what that is!' I shouted through the keyhole.

'Never you mind what it is!' he shouted back.

'It's blood! It's Nain's footprints!' I thought I was going to cry.

Seeing the footprints made me think–why *did* she walk up the mountain in her bare feet?

I heard the tap running as Dad wiped the floor.

He came out a few moments later with the tea. 'Don't go in there, it's slippery,' he said. 'We'll get our heads down and tomorrow we can all go together to see her.'

'We could take turns,' I said, 'so that there's someone with her all the time.'

'I'm not going,' Caroline said. 'Old people are so…'

Dad looked at her from under his eyebrows. 'What?'

'...scary. Like they've had a bad Botox job.'

'Oh yes, very scary,' Dad said sarcastically. His voice softened. 'You've got to come. She'll be asking where you are.'

'I'll sleep on it,' Caroline said.

She was still sleeping on it next morning when we got up.

Dad and I ate Nain's Cornflakes. 'We'll have to write a list of what we need to replace,' he said. While I wrote 'Buy More Cornflakes' and 'Milk' on the back of an envelope, he rang the care home.

After breakfast, we went to see her. The care home was called Whitehill and it was a mile from the village. I don't know why it was called that. There was no hill, just a big old house with a wall around it and leafy oak trees lining the drive. There was a sign for the Car Park, and another saying Visitors' Entrance.

I went through the front door expecting the place to be full of nurses, beds, patients, flowers and grapes; that sort of thing. Instead, it was gloomy, like a big old hotel. There was a large desk by the side of a winding staircase. A woman with shiny brown hair in a pony-tail was sitting by a desk, looking through papers. A brass sign in front of her said: SIAN LLEWELYN.

She was wearing a long, dark blue dress with long, dangling sleeves, and she lifted her head and smiled as if she was really happy to see us. 'Hello! Who have you come to visit?'

'Branwen Jones. I'm Michael, her son,' Dad said. 'And this is Ava.'

'You go on up,' Sian Llewelyn said to me. 'She's in the Day Room. Up the stairs, and press the buzzer on the yellow door to let yourself in.'

'There's a buzzer?'

'For security reasons. They wander, you see.'

Maybe all old people headed towards the mountains, I thought as I climbed the stairs. I imagined holding open the doors for them and setting them free.

The Day Room was as bad as the downstairs – gloomy, full of old people in antique chairs with their backs against the walls. Facing them was a large, bright plasma tv, showing Scrubs.

15

And that's the moment when the old man asked me if I wanted to know a secret, and I said yes.

Chapter Three

The first weird thing I noticed about Nain was that her white hair was wild and she was wearing a horrible pink cardigan that was buttoned all wrong. That's not like her at all.

'Hello, Nain,' I said, kissing her and nearly knocking off her wire-rimmed glasses. I pulled up a chair and stared at her poor bandaged feet. 'Do they hurt?'

'It's like walking on nettles! What are you doing here?'

'It's the school holidays,' I reminded her.

'I know that,' she said irritably.

That's what you get for being helpful. 'Oh, sorry. I thought you had dementia.'

'Ha ha! That's the idea!' she said, looking incredibly pleased with herself. She winked at me. 'I'm pretending I've lost my mind. The good thing is, everyone believes me. They do, when you're my age.'

'You're pretending? But why?'

Nain looked at me over her glasses. 'Because, Ava, it was the only way I could get myself admitted. I have to keep Idrys over there from telling secrets that he's supposed to keep to himself.'

I looked across at the old man. The blue light from the television was shining on his bald head and his lips fluttered with his snores. 'You mean the secret about the severed Head?'

'You're not supposed to know that,' Nain said crossly. 'You've only been here five minutes.'

One thing you ought to know about me is that I'm always arguing. 'Don't blame me! If you've come in here to stop him talking, you haven't done a very good job.'

'I know,' Nain admitted. She looked around quickly to check no-one was listening and she lowered her voice. 'Don't worry. I've got a plan.'

I didn't like the sound of that. 'Are you going to kill him?'

'Don't be silly,' she said sharply. 'I'm going to get him out of here before he gets the whole world looking for the Head. Not a word to your father, you hear?'

As if! I never tell him anything I don't have to. 'He'll wander,' I warned.

There was a buzz, and the Day Room door opened.

I hoped it was Dad, but it wasn't. It was a boy about my own age. He was a Goth and he was wearing a black baggy t-shirt and black jeans. Half his head was shaved almost bald, while the other side his hair was long and fair, flopping over one eye. He looked as if he'd gone to have his hair cut and changed his mind halfway through.

He looked my way and he waved at me.

I felt my face get pink. 'He's waving at me!'

'No, he's waving at me.' Nain waggled her fingers back at him.

The boy crouched over Idrys and tapped him awake. Idrys opened his eyes and looked at the corners of the ceiling as if he was checking for cobwebs.

The boy folded his arms and the muscles moved under his skin.

I shivered. 'Who is he, Nain?'

'Tal,' she said. 'Nice boy.'

'Nice? Really?'

'He's the son of Fred Evans, the poet from Tŷ Mawr,' she said, as if that explained everything.

The old man held out his bony hands and Tal reached out to help him to his feet. Suddenly the old man grabbed his wrist and twisted. With a struggle, Tal pulled himself free and rubbed his arm.

'Nain! Idrys gave him a Chinese burn!'

'Poor Idrys,' Nain said. 'His mind comes and goes.'

I was trying to imagine what that was like when the old man shouted:

'FIND ME THE HEAD OF BRÂN!'

He startled the old people. The men started to swear and the women started to cry. It was as noisy as school.

'Ah me!' the old man next to us said loudly, reaching for me and nearly falling out of his chair, 'Myfanwy? Is that you?'

'No, sorry.'

Tal was pulling at the door handle to escape, but it was locked.

I know how I'd feel if I'd started a riot in an old people's home, and I hurried over to help him. 'You have to ring the buzzer,' I said, 'and they'll open it.'

'I know.' He pressed the buzzer and flicked his fair hair out of his eyes.

'The old man gave you a Chinese burn, didn't he?'

'Yeah.'

'Is he your grandad?'

'No,' he said. He pressed the buzzer again. 'His name's Idrys Hughes. He's my teacher.' He rubbed his hand across his face. 'It's like Night of the Living Dead in here. The old people look the same but they're not. Their eyes are different.'

He was right; it *was* like the Night of the Living Dead. 'It's dementia,' I said quickly.

'Yeah, I know that.'

The sadness in his voice made me feel better.

'Now he's taking his clothes off,' Tal said, staring over my shoulder. 'Don't look.'

I always have to look when someone says that; I don't know why. The old man had unbuttoned his jacket and he struggled to pull his arm out of his sleeve.

'I hate it when he does that.'

'So why are you visiting him, then?'

'It's complicated. He's lost his memories and I have to find out something,' the boy said again, this time keeping his hand on the buzzer. I could hear it ringing in the distance.

A woman in a white overall hurried to the door and popped into the day room.

'At it again, is he?' she asked sympathetically. 'Get dressed, Idrys,' she called over cheerfully. 'It's morning, bach!'

For a moment the old man looked thoughtful. Then his face cleared. 'Morning, is it?' He began to fasten his jacket again.

I followed Tal to the top of the stairs and he swung the seat out of the red Stannah Stairlift. 'Want a ride?'

I laughed and glanced towards the yellow door of the Day Room. I hadn't said goodbye to Nain, but honestly I was glad to get out of there.

I sat on the fold-up seat while Tal hung on the back and slowly the chair moved down on its track. He leapt off before the bottom of the stairs and ran to undo the catch on the door.

When he opened it, I could smell the grassy summer air rush into the dark house, cool and fresh and clean. There was no sign of Dad or Sian Llewelyn the care home manager, so I followed Tal out and closed the main door carefully behind me.

Tal stopped on the grass a few yards down the drive.

He was watching one of the oak trees intently, his brown arms dangling by his side.

'Look,' he said, pointing.

A bird croaked harshly from under the canopy of green leaves. Pruuuk!

Up in the branches I could see smooth blue-black feathers, a cruel, curved beak and the glint of a dark eye. Even half-hidden, the bird looked huge, but the strangest thing about it was that even though we were staring at it, it didn't move at all. It just sat in the branches watching us, as still as if it was stuffed.

'What is it?' I whispered. 'A crow?'

Tal didn't answer.

I clapped my hands, hoping the bird would fly away. It didn't. It cocked its head and looked at me through its other eye. 'What's it doing?' I whispered nervously.

Tal turned to look at me. His fringe half-hid his eyes and he took a black beanie out of his pocket and jammed it on his hair. With his half-shaved bristles hidden, he looked more normal. His eyes were pale, so grey that they looked transparent, and I blinked.

'What's blacker than a raven's wing?' he asked me.

I shrugged.

'It's a riddle,' Tal said. 'Idrys told it to me.'

'So what's the answer?'

'Death.'

'That's not funny.'

'It's not supposed to be. Ravens eat carrion. Flesh,' he added. 'They wait around battlefields to feed off the dead.'

'Disgusting.'

'It's in a poem by Taliesin,' he said seriously. '"From warriors, ravens grew red."'

'Shut up,' I said irritably because he was beginning to freak me out. 'I'm going home. I'll see you around.'

'Idrys is going to die,' he called after me.

I thought of Nain and her plan and I shivered. 'Well he's old,' I called back, and I started walking quickly towards the gates. My heart was beating fast and everything seemed nasty because Nain was in the care home and she was old too.

I started to run. When I reached the gates, I turned back.

Tal was still staring up at the tree. And something strange happened.

The thing is, there were lots of trees along the drive, and it was summer so they were covered in green leaves. There were about twenty huge oaks between me and Tal, but as I stood by the gate I could clearly see the raven on the distant branch, and not just part of it, but all of it, from its sharp beak and its beady eye to its gleaming tail, the whole thing.

I couldn't work out how I could see it so plainly.

And at some stage, the sun must have shone right into my eyes, it must have. Because when I finally blinked, the bird turned red as blood.

Chapter Four

Next morning I was woken up by Caroline yelling as if she was being murdered.

I sat up in Nain's spare bed in the attic room in a state of shock. 'Caroline?'

'Ava! Come quickly!'

There were a few things I had forgotten to pack, including a dressing gown, so I put Nain's on – blue towelling on the inside and multi-coloured silk on the outside – and hurried downstairs. 'What's happening?'

Caroline was standing by the window in a pink velvet dressing gown, waving her hand to me. 'Cows! Quick! Get me the phone!'

The cows were in the garden, twelve black and white Friesians. They were huddled by the window, looking at us – cows are curious and I think Caroline's scream had attracted them. I gave her the phone. 'Are you going to ring the farmer?'

'I'm calling the police.'

'What are the police going to do, arrest them?'

Caroline stared at me for a moment and didn't say anything. Then she put her spare hand in her pocket and took out a small packet of Nicorette, popped one out and started to chew urgently. 'So what would you do?'

We looked at the cows, and the cows looked at us. The nearest one stuck out its blue tongue and licked the glass.

'That's disgusting,' Caroline said, staring at the drool. 'Ava - where are you going?'

'I'm going to get rid of them.'

'How?'

I rolled my eyes.

'Don't do anything stupid,' Caroline said. 'Don't corner them!'

'They're not zombie killer cows, you know,' I said and went into the kitchen and opened the back door. Clapping my hands, I shouted to the cows to go home. The one that licked the window made a little sideways jump and headed for the gate and the others followed with their heads down as though they'd been told off.

The lawn looked a mess and some of the red tiles on the path had broken under their weight.

I went back in to write the damage on the list of things to do: Repair Path and Wipe Cow Spit Off Window.

'I can't believe you did that,' Caroline said as I propped it up on the mantelpiece.

'I can't believe you're scared of cows. Where's Dad?'

'He's gone to buy a newspaper and some deodorant.' Caroline was filling the kettle. 'Stupid place,' she said, turning off the tap. 'I hate the country. There's too much space, too many trees. And the birds are too big.' She plugged the kettle in. 'There was one here this morning, it was that size.' She spread her arms wide.

'Was it an ostrich?' I asked helpfully.

'It wasn't an ostrich, it was black.'

I caught my breath as I thought of the raven. 'Was it a – ' I started to ask, but it's not as if Caroline would know.

'Coffee?' she asked.

'Yes, please.'

She brought the coffees to the table and we sat there in our dressing gowns, staring at each other through the steam.

'So how did Branwen look to you yesterday?'

I thought about Nain's fake dementia. 'Okay, I suppose.'

'Good. If she looked okay I'm going back to London.'

'When?'

'Tomorrow. Michael says he's staying on but two days of birds and cows is enough for me.'

I broke her gaze and stared at the shiny black coffee instead.

I never drank coffee before I met Caroline but when she was making one for herself, she'd make me one too. She just assumed I liked it. And I sort of do now.

If I could have chosen a future Step, it wouldn't be Caroline, that's for sure. Life is very calm with Dad, so calm that we go for hours without talking. Caroline's the opposite. She's always arguing about something or other. She's a bit like me for that. But I like her in a funny way. If we were in a boating accident and they were drowning and I could only save one of them, I would of course save Dad. But I would certainly try to save Caroline as well.

'How long do you think Dad's going to stay for?' I asked after a few minutes.

'Until her feet heal. That's what he said.' She took her chewing gum out of her mouth and stuck it on the coaster. 'How long would that take? Couple of weeks?'

'Yeah,' I said. 'A couple of weeks. Max.'

'Too long.'

We looked at each other.

Whitehill gave me the creeps. I could always come back when Nain came home, once her feet were cured.

'I'm not babysitting you, if that's what you're thinking,' Caroline said, pointing a teaspoon at me.

'I haven't had a babysitter since I was ten.'

Caroline shrugged. It was settled. I was going home with her.

Just then, Dad came back from his shopping trip with a Daily Telegraph, six croissants and a jar of blackcurrant jam but he'd forgotten the deodorant.

I didn't say anything about it because I'd decided on a plan. I was going to be the ideal daughter for the whole day so that when I asked if I could go back with Caroline, he would have to say yes.

After breakfast Dad and I started up the road to go and see Nain again while Caroline stayed in bed.

It was another warm, sunny day so I pushed the sleeves of my red t-shirt up in the hope of getting a tan. As we rounded the corner I saw someone coming slowly towards us, keeping in the shadows of the hedge. He was wearing a black suit and a black waistcoat. It was Idrys. Nain's daring plan had worked! Honestly, I've never been so proud.

'Well look who it is!' Dad said suddenly, shielding his eyes from the sun. 'Hullo, Idrys!'

Uh-oh.

'Hello, Michael,' the old man said.

'Escaped, have you?' Dad joked.

'Aye,' Idrys replied, coming out of the shade into the sunlight. 'You could say that.'

He was just about to walk past us when Dad blocked his way.

'Just a minute,' Dad said. 'Does Sian Llewelyn know where you are?'

'I don't rightly know.'

'Look,' Dad said, rubbing his chin, 'you're not supposed to be out on your own. Tell you what, let's walk back to Whitehill together, shall we, nice and easy. We're going that way ourselves, aren't we, Ava?'

I didn't know why he was bringing me into it - I was on Nain's side. If Dad started meddling, he was going to ruin everything. 'You can't make him go back if he doesn't want to,' I pointed out. 'He's a grown man.'

'That's true enough,' Idrys said, standing a bit straighter. 'Michael, let me pass. I have business to take care of.'

'Business? What business?'

'A most extraordinary business,' Idrys said eagerly. 'Do you want to know a secret?'

Arghhhh! I could imagine a million ways that my father could waste that Head. He'd probably use it to ask for a new lawnmower.

Luckily my dad is nothing like me.

'No thanks,' he said. 'I'm not big on that sort of thing.'

Idrys stood helpless in his buttoned-up black jacket. 'In that case, you have to trust me,' he pleaded. 'Please?'

Little did he know my dad doesn't trust anyone. He's the most suspicious person I've ever met. He took Idrys's arm firmly in his.

'I'm sorry, but for your own good I'm taking you back to Whitehill.'

'Let me go - ' Idrys struggled to get his arm free but he had no chance. Since Dad met Caroline, he's been working out. His biceps are like rocks.

'Yes,' I said, 'let him go!' I was angry with Dad. 'You're a bully and you're ruining everything! Nain's going to be furious.'

Idrys was flapping wildly. Suddenly I caught my breath. Something strange was happening to him. His face seemed to be changing before my eyes. The skin was folding in deep grooves from his nose to his jaw and his nose looked different – sharper, somehow. He screwed up his eyes in concentration and with his free hand he started unfastening the buttons of his black jacket.

Here he goes, I thought nervously, but he suddenly lifted his elbow high, forearm hanging, making a harsh, aggressive noise in his throat as he wheeled towards Dad like a huge bird.

My heart raced in panic – boomboomBOOM – and Dad jumped about a foot in the air.

I couldn't blame him. Idrys was a scary sight, perched on the pavement, arms raised, head cocked, black jacket flapping like wings in the summer breeze. His eyes were so fierce and dark that I couldn't see the whites. He jerked towards Dad who backed away at top speed. I had no idea he could move that fast.

When he was a safe distance away, Idrys lowered his arms. Now that his face wasn't in shadow, the sunshine lit it up and his eyes, I could see now, were not black and beady – they were clear and kind.

Dad stayed where he was, looking pale. He wiped his sweaty forehead with his hand. 'Well, we'll be off then, Idrys,' he said casually, pretending nothing had happened. 'Nice to see you. Come on, Ava.'

'I'd better go,' I told Idrys. 'Good luck!'

When I reached Dad, he asked me, 'Do you feel okay?'

'Yes, why?'

'I think the croissants were off. I thought for one moment Idrys was going to – ' He frowned and stopped himself.

'Peck you?'

'Don't be stupid!' he said.

'His nose went pointy – '

'Ava – '

'He looked like a – '

'SHUT UP!'

I did.

I've never seen Dad so angry in my life.

'It's indigestion, that's all,' he said after a moment. 'He's just a – ' He glanced down the road, frowning. 'He's just an old man, wandering. I suppose we should keep an eye on him, see where he goes. I'll follow him and you go and tell Sian Llewelyn that he's got out.'

I turned back to look at Idrys. He was almost by the church. He'd gone a long way in a short time. I was sure Dad wouldn't be able to move that fast but I couldn't take the risk.

'Tell you what - you tell Sian Llewelyn, and I'll follow him,' I suggested instead.

Dad looked slightly more cheerful. 'But don't antagonize him,' he warned.

As if I would! I was totally on Idrys's side. But I didn't bother answering, because Idrys was almost out of sight as he passed the church wall. I knew that the road led to the mountains, and I started to run.

Chapter Five

I ran as fast as I could past Nain's, through the village and past the church but I couldn't catch up with Idrys.

I had a stitch and I stopped to get my breath and stared at the empty narrow road that led towards the mountains.

As I headed back I looked in the church yard, just in case. But he wasn't there, so with a clear conscience I ran all the way up to Whitehill to tell Dad he'd vanished. A van zoomed past me as I reached the oak trees in the drive. I was hot, sweaty and thirsty.

By the main entrance I could see Dad and Sian talking, and her shiny brown pony tail was ruffling in the breeze. She was really pretty and I noticed that Dad wasn't grumpy with her.

'We're so security-aware… it's a complete mystery how he managed to get out,' she was saying.

Dad saw me. 'Here she is!' he said, pointing.

They both turned to look at me hopefully.

I hobbled the last few metres because I had cramp. 'Sorry, I don't know where he went, I couldn't catch him up,' I said truthfully.

'What?' Sian Llewelyn was suddenly annoyed. 'What do you mean, you couldn't catch him up? The man is seventy-five years old!'

'But he was really fast. He was bouncing along, wasn't he Dad?'

'He did seem in a hurry,' Dad agreed.

Sian's fingers dug into my arm. 'Where was he going?'

'I don't know,' I said, pulling myself free.

'You don't know?' She turned on Dad. 'This is your fault, Michael,' she spat. 'You should have rung me instead of wasting time running after him all over the place. It's a very serious matter, you know.'

Now Dad was annoyed, too - he wasn't used to being told off. 'You ought to think about checking your security before you blame me. He was in your care, after all. If he can get out, anyone can.'

Sian Llewelyn and my dad glared at each other.

'They wander,' Sian said. But she obviously decided that Dad had a point, because after a few moments she forced a smile. 'I will double check our security. Your mother's safe here, I can assure you of that. And the doctor's coming for her feet this morning.'

Yuk!

'Good,' Dad said, and we went into the gloomy care home.

The Stannah Stairlift was folded against the wall and Dad and I walked up together and buzzed ourselves in through the yellow door.

The room was exactly the same as the day before – the huge television glowed bright and blue against the far wall, and people sat around the room mumbling, staring into the huge, dark, carpeted space between them.

Nain was wearing the horrible bright pink cardigan again.

'Your plan worked. We saw Idrys on the road,' I said softly, 'and Sian Llewelyn's furious!'

'I bet she is,' Nain said.

I couldn't tell her anything more because Dad sat down next to her.

I was hot from all the running around, and really thirsty, so I told them I was going to get a drink. I went downstairs to look for Sian Llewelyn, but there was no-one around, and so I decided to go to the kitchen for a glass of water. The kitchen was large, clean and bare, with lots of stainless steel. The cupboards were locked so I leant over the sink and held my hair back to drink from the tap.

'Hey! What are you doing?'

I wiped my mouth and turned round.

A gorgeous dark-haired boy wearing a khaki t-shirt and baggy camouflage trousers was standing in the doorway, holding a broom like a shotgun. He had dark blue eyes and the thickest, darkest eyelashes I had even seen.

'You're not supposed to be in here,' he said.

'I'm thirsty.' I wiped my hands on my jeans. My face was still hot from running so I knew my face was as red as my t-shirt. 'I've been looking for Idrys.'

'Oh yeah? How do you know Idrys?'

'I saw him yesterday in the day room and then my dad and I saw him on the road and my dad tried to stop him, but he let him go in the end,' I said, all in one breath.

The guy propped his broom against the wall. 'He's lost his mind. Maybe he's gone looking for it.' He grinned and held out his hand. 'I'm James Dodd.'

'Ava Jones.'

'Ava Jones,' he mimicked me. 'Where are you from, then? London?'

'Yes.'

He smirked. 'I thought so. London,' he said scornfully.

'What's wrong with London?'

'There's plenty wrong with it.' He pulled the neck of his khaki t-shirt, which was dark with sweat. 'You remember those London bombers? The ones on the Tube? I met those guys when I was a kid.'

'No, you didn't.'

'Yeah I did. They were up in Bala on my mate's dad's land. I bet you a tenner I met them.'

'Why would I bet you a tenner?'

His grin widened. 'See? You do believe me.'

'It's not funny. Bombers kill people,' I said, getting annoyed. 'It's nothing to be proud of.'

'Isn't it? BOOOM!'

I jumped, and he laughed.

I hated him. 'You're an idiot,' I said, and I walked out.

Back in the day room, Dad and Nain were watching *The Simpsons*. Dad was slumped in his chair looking sleepy; practising being an old man.

Nain took my hand, and pulled me to face her. She had her glasses on, so I could see the television reflecting blue, white and red in the lenses but I couldn't see her eyes.

'Nain?'

'What, Ava?'

'How did you get Idrys out?' I whispered.

Nain's eyes were watery blue. 'My room overlooks the car park. I took him into my room, and helped him out of my bedroom window onto the kitchen roof and down the drainpipe. Easy!'

It sounded dangerous to me, especially for old people. I glanced at my dad, who was staring at the tv in a trance. His mouth was open and his eyes were wide and blank. He ought to have been paying attention - I mean, she was his mother. 'I'm not being negative but I don't think your plan's going to work. Idrys is still talking about the Head. He almost told Dad, for a start. For all you know, he might have told lots of people and someone might already be using the magic Head as we speak.'

'It's not a magic Head. It's a holy relic.'

'What's a relic?'

'Holy bones with supernatural powers. You remember St. Winifred's well?'

'Oh yeah... those bones that can cure you, right?'

Nain looked at me sternly over her glasses. 'And in this case, Ava, it also protects this country.'

I shrugged. Sounded the same as a magic Head to me.

Nain took her spectacles off and fluffed up her white hair until it stuck out like a dandelion clock. She does that when she's thinking. 'I've got a little job for you.'

'Cleaning out the shed?'

'No. You've got to go to Tŷ Mawr to help Tal. Now that Idrys has got away he's on his own, and two heads are better than one.'

Honestly, I was sick of hearing about heads. And I've got enough to do with homework. 'But I don't even like Tal!' I folded my arms. 'And I can't, because Caroline said I could go back to London with her and come back when your feet are better.'

Nain screwed her mouth up tight and picked up her steel-framed spectacles from her lap and put them back on. End of conversation.

In her glasses I could see twin reflections of the television. Marge was driving Homer's pink car, her blue hair squashed at right angles against the roof.

And then, something scary happened.

The scene in the glasses changed.

In one lens I could see a grinning skull glowing with light, and for a moment flesh and hair came and went and I could see the face over the skull. Suddenly there was an explosion of red heat and smoke. I could see the black outline of buildings I recognised – St. Paul's Cathedral, the Shard and the Tower of London. My face was burning with the heat and my heart thumped as I turned around quickly to look at the television, thinking it was a newsflash. But it was still The Simpsons - Marge with her bright blue hair, driving towards a cliff top.

I looked at Nain again and the fire was still burning in her spectacles. 'Give me your glasses,' I said, but when she handed them to me the lenses were cool and clear.

I looked through them carefully from all angles. I folded them and unfolded them. Then I put them on my nose and stared at the blurred carpet. What can I tell you? They were just ordinary glasses. 'How did you do that?'

'I'm a druid,' Nain said proudly.

I folded the glasses up. 'I know.' Druids are philosophers and poets and doctors and lawyers and teachers, and they live in harmony with nature and read the future in bird flights and that sort of thing. But no-one ever mentioned they could do the glasses trick. If Nain had told me about that, I'd have paid more attention.

'And also Rowan Williams, the last Archbishop of Canterbury is a druid. And so is Idrys and Sian Llewelyn and so was Winston Churchill and William Blake and –'

'Okay, I get it.'

'– so is Tal.'

I stared at her. 'Tal? *Tal* is?'

'Well, he's only young and he's still learning. Idrys is his teacher. But now he's going to need a friend. Someone with brains, who's not afraid to use them.'

It took a couple of seconds before I realised she meant me.

'But Nain -' I protested, and her glasses started to warm up in my hands. Suddenly I had a bad feeling that if I looked at them I would see London burning again. I stopped arguing, handed them back quickly, and stood up. 'Fine! I'll go!'

Chapter Six

Tŷ Mawr is Welsh for Big House. It's just off the road to the hills, and in the daytime it's quite hard to see because it's surrounded by trees.

It was quite a long walk. I had to go back past Nain's, and past the church again, and over a stream and up a narrow road. All I could hear was sheep. I'd had more exercise that day than I usually have in a week.

I opened the big metal gate and walked up the drive and rang the bell, trying to work out what to say to Tal and hoping that he wasn't in.

But he was. He opened the door and peered at me through his fair fringe.

'Oh,' he said, 'it's you.'

'My Nain sent me. Don't even ask me why.'

He grinned. 'Okay then, I won't. Idrys is here.'

So that's why I hadn't found him!

I followed Tal into a huge lounge overlooking the garden. Idrys was sitting in a gold armchair framed in sunlight and he raised his hand to greet me. He smiled and rubbed his jaw thoughtfully and his bristles whispered against his fingers. He cast a long, dark bird shadow on the carpet.

'Sian Llewelyn's furious that you've gone,' I warned him.

'No doubt.'

'You know about the Head, don't you,' Tal said to me.

'Kind of. Whose head is it, anyway?'

Tal's gaze rested on mine for a moment. 'A guy named Brân. He was King of Siluria. It's where Gwent is now. He was a great leader and he was captured by the the Romans and taken to Rome where he met St. Paul in prison and got converted.'

'So how did he lose his head?'

'He was fighting in a terrible battle when he got stabbed in the foot by a poisoned arrow. He asked his men to cut his head off.'

I frowned. 'Why didn't they just cut off his foot?'

'He was injured. You can't lead men if you're injured, can you? He knew they couldn't save him so he wanted them to kill him. And he made them a promise that his Head would look after them even after he was dead.'

It was the saddest story ever when I thought about it.

All during the battle you'd be scared of getting killed, and then you just get injured and you think, great, it's only my foot, it's only a poisoned dart, I can hop around on crutches or something, and then you realise it makes no difference because you're finished anyway and so you have to make your mates cut off your head. It didn't seem fair.

'How come I've never heard of him before?'

'You can't have everyone knowing about a holy Head, can you?' Tal said. 'It's supposed to be a secret.'

We both tried not to look at Idrys.

The old man sighed. 'And because of me, the secret is out and the Head is in jeopardy now.' He moved his fingers and the shadow-bird lifted its wings. He looked at me carefully and his blue eyes were so bright that I blinked. 'Do you believe in visions, Ava?'

I was surprised by the question. 'No,' I said. 'Certainly not.' I might have seen something strange in Nain's glasses, but it didn't mean I believed in them.

I hugged my elbows. If I helped Tal find the Head I could test out its powers before giving it back.

Genius! I surprise myself, sometimes; I really do. 'So have you remembered where it is now?'

'He knows,' Idrys said, pointing to Tal.

Tal was startled. 'No, I don't! I'll never find it! And you can't help me, can you, Idrys? I know the answer to the riddle, I know what's darker than a raven's wing. It's death. You're going to die.'

'True,' Idrys said. 'But I want to die. Don't worry about me. I'm not afraid of going to the Otherworld. I have friends who have gone before me who owe me money from this life and I'll be a rich man when I get there. I'm old and I'm not myself any more. My death will make you stronger.'

Tal's blonde hair flopped into his eyes and he cupped his chin in his hand. 'How can your death make me stronger?' he asked helplessly. 'I'm too young to stop bad things happening. I don't know what to do, or how to do it.'

Idrys rested his veined hand gently on Tal's shoulder. 'Memory loss makes a good case for the written word,' he said ruefully. 'You'll know what to do, I'm sure. You've had eight years of learning and while your knowledge isn't complete, it should be sufficient. It will have to be.'

'Just a minute, hold up there,' I said, because I'd been thinking hard. 'If you guys don't know where the Head is, and nobody else knows where it is, it means it's safe, right? I can go back to London?'

'Alas, no.' Idrys's bird-shadow folded its wings and faded as a cloud slid over the sun. 'If the Head is in danger then the country is in danger, and haven't we seen for ourselves visions of London roaring in flames, unprotected?'

I jumped; I couldn't help it.

Idrys looked up and for a moment I saw something rippling against the ceiling like a reflection. His face became softer, the skin paler, the wrinkles deeper as he frowned. The room was deadly quiet. Idrys said to Tal, lowering his voice, 'Keep it safe, my boy. You need to look into the Druids' Book to find its whereabouts.'

'There's a book?' Tal was surprised. 'Where?'

'You know where the book is,' the old man said softly. 'The book is bound in human flesh.'

He rubbed his temples as if he had a migraine. The sun came out again, and the shadow darkened on the carpet. It was the shadow of an old man.

Tal was worried. 'Are you okay?'

Idrys got to his feet and shook his head to clear it. 'I have to go now.'

'Look,' Tal said urgently, tugging his sleeve, 'I don't know where the book is or what it looks like or anything. Please don't go. You've got to help me here, Idrys.'

With effort, Idrys moved towards the door.

'Don't go!'

Idrys turned to him. He looked sad and puzzled and then he opened the door cautiously and waited a moment.

He looked up and down the empty driveway and left without saying goodbye.

We stood in the doorway and watched him as he walked slowly up the road towards the hills, his black jacket flapping brokenly around him.

When he was out of sight, Tal closed the door.

'What's the book that's bound in human flesh?' I asked him. 'It sounds disgusting.'

'I don't know about any book.'

'Idrys says you do.'

'Well he's wrong,' Tal said, and he started picking a scab on his arm. 'I've never seen it in my life, and I should know.'

'I wonder where Idrys is going.'

'He's going to the hills to the Otherworld. He was my teacher,' Tal said. He rubbed his cheek and stood up. He went over to the window, resting his elbows on the sill.

'But you've got other teachers, haven't you?' I asked.

'No. I've never been to school. It's just him.'

I tried to imagine never going to school. I wouldn't miss my teachers but I would definitely miss my friends.

After a couple of minutes I had a bad feeling Tal was crying so I tried to think of something to say that would make him feel better. In films, people always say, 'It's going to be fine,' but I couldn't say that because it wasn't true. We had to find a book somewhere that was bound in real skin, and we had to protect a Head, and Idrys, the only person who could help us, had gone wandering to the hills to die.

Chapter Seven

'Where the hell have you been?'

That's what Dad said when I got back to Nain's. He was all red and annoyed.

'I went to Tal's. Nain told me to.'

'Oh? And I suppose if she told you to poke yourself in the eye with a pencil, you would, would you?'

What???

'I've been trying to call you! Why is your phone switched off?'

'Because I've run out of credit from ringing Rosie.'

'You went off without a word!' He was unstoppable.

I remembered I was trying to be good for the day so he'd let me go back with Caroline, so instead of storming out with my arms folded as I usually did, I took a deep breath. 'I'm sorry I worried you, Dad.'

He looked confused.

'The thing is, even though you were watching The Simpsons I thought you'd heard us talking. Sorry,' I said again.

'Well – that's all right. I'm sorry I yelled.'

'That's okay.' I felt quite kindly towards him, especially as he was starting to look normal once more.

'It's the worry,' he said. 'There's no sign of Idrys and Sian is taking it hard.'

'Who's Sian?' Caroline asked, popping up to look at us. Her blonde hair was piled up and held in place with two chopsticks.

'She's in charge of Whitehill,' I said. 'She's pretty. She's got long, shiny hair.'

Caroline sat even straighter. 'Really.' She thought for a moment. 'How old is she?'

'Oh,' Dad said, 'she's quite old, isn't she, Ava?'

'Yeah, she's at least twenty-five.'

'TWENTY-FIVE? Right,' Caroline said, 'it's about time I paid Nain a visit.'

'She'll enjoy that,' Dad said happily, as though he believed it.

'Dad, I'm going back to London with Caroline,' I said, getting it in quickly while he was cheerful. 'She said I could.'

Caroline frowned. 'No, I didn't.'

'You didn't say I couldn't.'

'I said I wasn't babysitting you.'

56

Yes. She did say that. 'But – '

'You're too young to stay at home on your own, Ava,' Dad said, 'as you very well know.'

'Anyway,' Caroline said, 'I'm staying here a bit longer.'

'Why? I thought you hated it here.'

She changed the subject. 'How anyone can be in charge of a care home at the age of twenty-five I just don't know,' she said, eating a bit of dry cereal.

I wandered into the parlour and looked at Nain's bookcase. Next to his silver sporting trophies was a photo of Dad at his graduation. He was with my dead granddad, Gwynne. Dad was standing next to a blue Rolls Royce which wasn't his. His hair was long and ginger. Poor Dad. I don't know what Mum saw in him.

I sat on the floor and looked at the books. Nain loved books. One caught my eye – it was called 'The Word and the Flesh' by Alice Williams, but despite the title it wasn't bound in human flesh, it was a paperback. And a play.

I hugged my knees. In the last couple of days, a lot of strange things had happened. I'd seen a black raven turn red. I'd seen the Head of Brân and London burning in Nain's glasses. I'd seen a man turning himself into a bird to frighten my dad. Things had happened that would have sounded crazy if I hadn't seen them for myself.

For a moment a strange feeling went through me. What if we found the Head and saved the country? What would that feel like?

And what if we failed?

The hugeness of it hit me suddenly. It wasn't a dream. It was real and frightening and it scared me. I couldn't keep it to myself any longer. I had to tell. 'Dad!' I scrambled to my feet and ran into the dining room in a panic. 'Dad!'

Dad came out of the kitchen wiping his hands on his shorts and bumped into me.

'What?'

'Dad – Idrys has gone – he's gone to – he's going to -' I was that near to telling. In that moment I could save him, I knew it. Dad would tell Sian Llewelyn and Idrys would be back safe watching television in Whitehill by tonight. My heart was beating fast. I started to cry, and then I couldn't stop.

'Caroline!' Dad shouted. 'Bring a toilet roll!' He squeezed me tightly against his chest. 'She's upset,' he said. 'Thanks. Tear a bit off. Upset about what? About Idrys getting lost, I think. Here. Here.' He was dabbing my ear with toilet paper.

I rubbed my runny nose on him and my breath was coming in jerks.

'*I* didn't say anything to upset her!' he protested, 'I was in the kitchen! What did you say? Yes, get her a coffee. Or a tea. What? No, not wine! Coffee, then, if she likes coffee. A Nicorette? NO!'

I struggled out of his hug so that I could breathe, and he gave me lots of pink toilet roll to blow my nose on.

My ears popped and my eyes were stinging.

Caroline came back with a cup of black coffee. She put it on the table. She looked at me closely. She was sadder than I'd ever seen her before. 'Stay there,' she said after a moment. 'I've got just the thing. Don't worry.'

I sat on a pine dining room chair, waiting, and she came back and crouched in front of me with a gold concealer pen. 'Touche Eclat,' she said, giving it to me.

'Dab it on your nose. It will hide the redness.'

She sounded a bit like a mother, and my eyes filled with tears again.

The next morning, Dad had something to tell me.

'Ava,' he said, 'you have to be brave. We've had a call from Sian Llewelyn.'

I sat at the table.

'It's about Idrys. I'm afraid it's bad news.' He pushed a pink toilet roll towards me.

But I didn't feel like crying. I was all cried out from yesterday and I just wanted to know what had happened. 'How did he die?'

'He was old,' Dad said. 'When a creature is very old, its body wears out and – '

'Dad, I'm not five, you know.'

Dad took a deep breath, and sighed. 'Idrys walked up the mountain. He took his clothes off some time during the night. People do that when they've got hypothermia – they get extremely cold and they start shivering, and then after a while they stop shivering and start to feel hot.

And they take their clothes off and feel sleepy. They don't wake up.'

'Does it hurt?'

'I don't think so, no.'

'That's good.' I thought about it for a moment. 'How can you get hypothermia in summer?'

'It's cold up there, trust me. Especially when the mist comes down.'

I slowly ate a mouthful of soggy cereal. I imagined Idrys up the mountain feeling cold, then hot, then falling asleep and waking up happily somewhere else, in some other world, to claim the money he was owed from his friends.

After breakfast, I went to Tal's to tell him the sad news. He answered the door with a peanut butter Kit Kat in his hand. I love peanut butter Kit Kats.

'I'd give you a bite, only it's my breakfast,' he said.

'I had cereal. Have you heard about Idrys?'

'Yeah.'

'He took all his clothes off and got hypothermia.'

Tal gave a small smile. 'Well,' he said after a moment, 'he's been practising long enough.'

'I'm not going back to London after all,' I told him. 'My dad's girlfriend's changed her mind.'

Tal flicked his blonde fringe out of his eyes. 'Your dad's got a girlfriend? Doesn't your mum mind?'

'I don't think so.' I felt my face going red. I don't talk about my mum. 'She's not around at the moment.'

'She died?'

'No. She needed to find herself. She went to Nepal.'

'Why would she go to Nepal to find herself? Does she come from Nepal?'

'No, she comes from Watford. And she hasn't come back yet because she's building houses and a school.'

'Parents should grow up,' Tal said.

He went into the kitchen and came back with a couple of cans of Diet Coke. He threw one to me. When I opened it, it fizzed in my face.

'Sorry,' he said, and he laughed.

I grabbed his black t-shirt and wiped my face on it, and he twisted my arm behind my back. 'Tal, I'm spilling it! I'm spilling it! Owwww!'

He threw me on the gold sofa and drank his Coke down in one. Then he belched loudly.

I sipped from the can and we looked at each other. He definitely seemed different. 'Do your powers feel stronger now Idrys is dead?' I asked hopefully.

Tal flicked the ring pull. 'I don't know,' he said. 'I can't tell yet.'

'What? Why not? How come you can't tell? When will you know?'

'When I see the signs, I suppose.'

'What signs? Bigger muscles?'

Tal grinned suddenly, as if I'd said something funny. 'First I have to find the Druid's Book.'

'Let's go and look for it now,' I said.

If I was going to be involved, I wanted it over and done with so I could enjoy the holidays. I was like that with exams. I hated putting off revision. For weeks I would be really nervous and my best friend Rosie and I would swear to each other that we hadn't done any work, just to make ourselves feel worse. Rosie wanted to be a model, so she couldn't see the point of exams, except for maths so she wouldn't have to pay an accountant, but her parents gave her money if she passed, so she had to worry about losing that as well. Me, I had nothing to fear but failure. Then about a week before the exams, I'd get so fed up of being scared that I'd start revising like mad, day and night, drinking diet Red Bull and eating Sour Cream and Chives Pringles. Chives are good for you.

'There's no hurry.' Tal crushed the can in his hand.

I had a sudden brilliant idea. 'Hey! We could look on Amazon!'

Tal started to laugh. I've never seen anyone laugh like that. He shook his arms and legs, and jumped about the lounge, and then he lay on the floor behind the sofa, gasping for breath, drumming his feet on the floor. I knelt on the sofa and stared down at him, baffled. 'What's so funny?'

'You are,' he said finally, and then he sat up, giggling weakly.

I was pleased I'd made him laugh. Mostly I'd only ever seen him looking worried. 'Okay,' I said, 'let's make a list of places to look. Idrys said you knew where it was, so it must be somewhere obvious. Have you got a pen?'

'Why don't you just memorize it?'

'I might forget something.'

Tal raised his eyebrows, but he got up off the floor and went out of the room. He came back with a pen and some paper and gave it to me.

I cleared a space and wrote: PLACES TO LOOK FOR THE DRUID'S BOOK. 'Okay.' I tapped my chin with the pen. 'The first place we should look is Idrys's room at Whitehill. He might have hidden it in there. Or…in his old house.' As I wrote them down, Tal said,

'His house has been sold.'

'So? He might have left it behind for the new people. How big is the book?'

'I don't know,' Tal said. 'I've never seen it.'

'That means it could be any size.' I remembered something startling. 'I had a Bible once that was two and a half centimetres square,' I said.

'What's the point of that?' Tal asked.

'It was the smallest Bible in the world.'

'Have you still got it?'

'No, it was so small I lost it. But,' I added helpfully, 'the book we're looking for isn't lost, because Idrys said you know where it is. Can't you just remember?'

'No, I can't,' Tal said, 'because I don't know where it is, I've never seen it in my life and I didn't even know it existed until yesterday.'

'Okay. So we look in Idrys's room, and then in his old house.'

'You can't. There are new people living there,' Tal said.

'I'll ask them nicely,' I said, folding up the list. He was right, I could have memorized it. But I could always add to it when I had another idea.

Just then, the phone rang. Tal grabbed it. 'Y'ello?' he said casually. Then his voice went all polite and he sat up straight. 'Oh, hello. Thank you. Yes. Thank you. I know. Thanks. Yes?'

There's nothing worse than listening to half a phone call. It sounded like a woman on the other end and I strained my ears to listen.

'What? How much? A week? Really?' Tal looked suddenly happy. 'Oh no, it's okay, my parents won't mind. They've been wondering what to do with me now Idrys has gone. Yeah. Okay, I'll be there.' He put the phone down with a bang and punched the air. 'Guess what? I've got a job at Whitehill! Sian Llewelyn wants me to talk to the old people and she's going to pay me for it! It's because of Idrys,' he added. 'She said they thought a lot of him. She said they missed their chats.'

'When do you start?'

'Tomorrow.' He scratched his neck awkwardly and looked at me through his hair. 'The book might be at Whitehill,' he said. 'I could have a look for it, in between talking to people.'

'In between talking to the Living Dead, you mean.'

'I don't mind talking to anyone if I get paid. We'll look in Whitehill and you can go and talk to the people at Idrys's old house, see if he left it behind.'

So that was the plan.

Chapter Eight

I couldn't go to Idrys's old house that morning though, because Dad, Caroline and I drove up to the blue lagoon so that I could practise swimming.

The blue lagoon is a flooded slate quarry up the Panorama. The water is always blue, because of the colour of the slate. We parked the car by the Ponderosa Café and walked half a mile uphill on springy grass to get there. There are huge piles of slates everywhere. I ran from one to the other, looking. 'Here it is! Oh, no – over here!' until finally I found it.

Climbing down to the blue water is dangerous because it's steep and slippery, so I took my time and waited impatiently for Dad and Caroline. A few minutes later, Caroline's head appeared at the top of the quarry.

'Hurry up!' I said, waving.

She stared down the slope, folding her arms. 'Are you crazy? I'm not coming down there,' she called. 'It's too steep. I hate heights.'

Dad appeared. 'Hold onto me,' he said to her, sticking his arm out for her to grab. 'There you go. You're safe, now.'

Caroline hung on to him, and took little tiny steps in her heels until she was halfway down. Then she slipped and squealed and slid the rest of the way on her bottom. I scrambled out of the way in case she knocked me in.

'Ow, that really hurt,' she said, twisting around to check the damage. 'Ava! I could have fallen in! Why didn't you catch me?'

'*I* might have fallen in,' I said.

'So? You're going in anyway.'

'Yes, but I've got all my clothes on. What am I supposed to do? Walk back all wet?'

'You could have swum in your clothes and then worn your cozzie to go home. Look at the state of my jeans,' she said, and looked up. 'Oh no! Michael!!!'

Dad was lurching down the last bit of the slope in a panic. 'Look out! Look out!'

Caroline and I screamed as he galloped towards us but luckily he skidded and fell over just in time. He lay on his back, groaning. 'I've broken something,' he said. 'I hope it's not the flask.' He sat up, rubbing his back. 'I don't remember it being that steep before,' he said in an offended tone.

All our days out together are a bit like this.

We start getting ready quite happily. Dad's the first in the car, but Caroline's still in the bathroom doing her make-up. After a while he gets impatient and beeps the horn. Then he gets cross and comes in to find us, so I get in the car to make him feel better, and after a while I beep the horn and go back in. And then we all come out together, only Dad's forgotten something and has to go back for it and by then it's started to rain.

Other families seem to have a great time, laughing, eating sandwiches and playing rounders, but not us. On our days out we argue non-stop.

I unpacked the bag and took out my swimming costume. 'Turn round and don't look until I tell you,' I said, and I got changed quickly.

The water was cold. I paddled at the edge and stared at my wet, pink tingling feet.

'Police divers practice their diving here,' Dad told Caroline. 'It's very deep.'

It's true. The blue lagoon isn't like the sea. It doesn't shelve gradually. One minute you're standing in an inch of water, and the next minute it's up to your neck. I took a deep breath and jumped. The water closed over me, shockingly cold, and I went down, down, down, through blue water flecked with pale, floating bits, and then up, up, up until I broke the surface, my hair sticking to my face. 'It's freezing!' I shouted, and started swimming freestyle, thinking of gold medals.

'Not too far!' Dad yelled.

I don't know why he said that. If you go too far, you reach the other side. I duck-dived down. I love swimming underwater. It's the nearest feeling to flying. When I came back to the surface, I checked my watch, and timed how long I could hold my breath.

As I swam down again, the pool did seem bottomless. It turned from turquoise to dark blue to dark grey, and then black. I couldn't see anything below me, no rocks, no fish, nothing. I blew out all my breath in a stream of bubbles so that I wouldn't float up too quickly, but it was all really bleak. And suddenly, for some reason, I didn't feel safe and I got scared and kicked for the surface, black to grey to blue, and gasped in the air, swimming as fast as I could to the side and scrambling out in a panic, cutting my knee on a sharp piece of slate.

'Well done,' Dad said encouragingly. He took the flask out and shook it. 'Ooo, that's lucky,' he said.

He poured three black coffees and I hugged mine, shivering, and looked up at the blue sky. In the far distance above us I could see a black bin liner flying in the wind. It was amazing; better than any kite. It inflated and twisted and tumbled as if it was on an invisible string.

Dad saw me looking and he shielded his eyes to look at it. 'What's that?'

'A bin liner.'

'No,' he said, 'it's too big for a bin liner. It's a piece of tarpaulin. It must be floating on the thermals.'

Caroline put her Dior sunglasses on to look at it. 'It's a tornado,' she said after a moment.

Whatever it was, it was getting closer, and the closer it came, the bigger it was – much bigger than a bin liner or a tarpaulin. It was a funny feeling, sitting down in the quarry with a black thing coming up overhead, casting a shadow. It was like being in a jar that someone was putting the lid on.

As it got closer, I could see that it wasn't a solid thing at all, it was birds. Their wings were rustling the air so hard I could feel the draught from them.

Dad jumped to his feet. 'Bloody hell,' he said, and he never swears, 'it's a flock of starlings. See? See? They're chasing something – they're chasing that sparrow hawk!'

The sparrow hawk swooped into the quarry – I could see him clearly now, dark against the sides of the cliff. 'They're mobbing him!' Dad said. 'Look – there he goes!' The noise of the birds was high-pitched and deafening, and over it all I could hear the sparrow hawk screech in pain. Suddenly he dropped out of the sky like a stone and hit the water, causing waves that splashed our feet. The starlings swirled in a huge dark circle above us and then streamed out past the top of the quarry, curling at the end like a ribbon and as they left, the sun shone on us again.

A few feathers floated on the blue water, drifting like little boats.

'What does it mean?' I whispered.

'Obviously,' Dad said, clearing his throat, 'they felt threatened, and they attacked it.'

'Yeah, but – what does it mean?'

He put the lid carefully back on the flask. 'Why don't you have another swim?'

I felt like Caroline – I wanted to say, Are You Crazy??? There was no way I was going back in that water, no way at all – and not just because I might swim into a torn up sparrow hawk.

'It means something,' I insisted. 'Dad, why didn't you become a druid so you'd know these things?'

'I don't like the beards,' he said. Then he laughed, 'Or should it be the bards? Ha-ha!'

'Seriously?'

He looked thoughtful. 'Well, it's a vocation, isn't it? Like teaching, or studying medicine. You have to be dedicated to it; it takes years to learn how to be one so it has to be something you believe in.'

'Don't you believe in it?'

Dad picked up a piece of slate and skimmed it across the water. It bounced twice and sank. 'You don't want to listen to Nain too much,' he said firmly. 'You thought you saw a bin bag, I thought I saw tarpaulin and Caroline thought she saw a tornado. But what we were actually looking at was a flock of birds. And sometimes a flock of birds is just a flock of birds.' He looked at me, and waited until I met his gaze. 'Got it?'

I nodded. Obviously, I didn't believe him.

I asked Tal about it later, when I went to Whitehill. He was listening to Nain in the plasma-lit day room and getting paid for it.

As I sat next to them, listening for free, Nain was telling him how Idrys had hopped out of her window.

Tal was picking a crusty brown scab on his thumb. He flicked his hair out of his eyes and looked up at her. 'Did you know he was going to die?'

She patted his hand. 'Yes, but we're old, you see, and that's our strength. Don't look so surprised! Old age has its advantages. You should never judge a book by its cover. Do you hear me, Ava?'

'Yes. You've told me before.' I don't actually get it, though. Me, I always judge a book by its cover. That's the whole point of a cover, right?

'Well, don't forget it. I'll be home soon Ava,' she said brightly, 'and then we can go off on our jaunts, as usual. I know it must be boring for you, with me stuck in here.'

'Not really - we went to the blue lagoon this morning,' I said. I told them about the starlings and the sparrow hawk. I was going to make it sound dramatic, but instead I told them it just as I'd remembered it. I could still see the sparrow-hawk dropping from the sky.

Tal was rubbing his bristly scalp as he looked at me thoughtfully. 'How do you know it was a sparrow hawk?'

'My dad told me.' I added, 'It means something, doesn't it?'

'The starlings had to gang up, because one starling against a sparrow hawk wouldn't be a fair fight, would it?' He checked his watch and then he stood up. 'Ava,' he said casually, 'Sian Llewelyn takes a break around now.'

'So? Oh! Okay.' The hunt for the mystery book was back on. I glanced at the television. A couple of old people were watching it but most of them were sleeping peacefully, open-mouthed.

I stood up, too. We were going to take a look at Idrys's room.

The bedrooms were on the next floor up, and we took the stairs. At the top was a child's safety gate, which we stepped over to go into the long corridor with a blue carpet where the bedrooms were.

'This is it,' Tal said. The names of the patients were on the cream doors; all except Idrys's. His name had already gone from the little gold frame and he'd only been dead for a day.

Tal pushed the door open and we went in. The room looked bare. The bed had been stripped, and the old sheets were bundled on the floor, ready to be washed. On the locker was a blue plastic cup half-full of water and a smaller, clear plastic empty one. The only other furniture was a chair and a fitted wardrobe.

There was a grey Samsonite suitcase on the floor and Tal and I crouched over it. I opened it hopefully. 'Clothes,' I said, going through them. They smelled of after shave. I found a folder full of letters and get-well cards, but no books of any kind.

We checked the locker, but it was empty.

I checked the wardrobe. Nothing.

Tal lay on the floor and felt under the bed and I went over to the window and leaned on the windowsill. I looked at the tops of the oak trees in the drive, thinking about the Druid's Book. If it was full of valuable information, Idrys would have wanted to keep an eye on it, wouldn't he? He'd said that Tal knew where it was, but Tal swore he didn't. And I believed him. I mean, if he knew where it was, we wouldn't still be looking for it, would we?

My breath was steaming up the glass and I suddenly realised that words were appearing on it that I couldn't understand. 'Tal! Come here! It's a message!' The words were fading, and I breathed on the glass again. 'Look – gwine – gween – gwun – '

'Gwyn Fryn,' Tal said, leaning on my shoulder. 'It's Welsh.'

'What does it mean?'

'It means White Hill.'

'Oh.'

Together we breathed on the whole window until I felt dizzy, as if I'd been blowing balloons. Gwyn Fryn, Gwyn Fryn, Gwyn Fryn, Gwyn Fryn, Gwyn Fryn.

'He must have been really bored,' Tal said, getting his breath back.

I was disappointed that it wasn't a clue, but I wiped the glass with my hand so that no-one else could read it. 'The Book's not here,' I said, wiping my wet hand on my jeans. I took the list out of my pocket and crossed off Idrys's Room. It hadn't been much of a list to start with, and now there was only one thing left on it. 'What's Idrys's old address?'

'Six, Moreton Avenue. It's by the school. You know the school?'

'Yeah.' I did know the school. It was near a row of shops – the newsagents, the solicitors, an off-licence and a fish and chip shop that was never open when you fancied chips. It only opened at lunch time and in the evening. What's the point of opening at meal times? At meal times you have meals. It's between meals that you feel hungry, right?

I wrote the address on the back of my sheet of paper and I clipped the pen onto the neck of my t-shirt. I was putting the list back in my pocket as I opened the door to leave Idrys's room and - what a shock! I bumped into good-looking James Dodd wheeling a laundry hamper!

James was wearing his camouflage gear. He had a hard look on his face which scared the pants off me.

'What are you up to?' he asked softly, parking the hamper and looking at me through his long, dark eyelashes. 'Robbing the dead?'

'No! I just came to see Idrys's room, that's all.'

'Why? You didn't even know him.'

I started to blush. 'I knew him a bit,' I said.

James looked at me steadily. 'What's that in your pocket?'

'It's a shopping list.'

He held his hand out for it.

Uh-uh.

Suddenly, I thought of Caroline. I flicked my hair away from my face. 'You want my shopping list?' I asked him. 'You want to do it for me? You want to shop? Go on then!' I pulled it out of my pocket and waved it at him. 'Take it! Take it! Are you happy now?'

James didn't take it. He looked at me as if I was crazy. 'You're not supposed to be on this floor,' he said after a moment. 'It's for residents only.'

I put the list back in my pocket. 'Where does it say that?'

'On the lift door.'

'Oh,' I said, 'that explains it. I came up the stairs.'

'Come on,' he said, 'I'll take you back down.'

As the lift doors closed, a bluebottle flew in with us. I ducked as it buzzed around but James grabbed it out of the air and cupped his hands around it. 'Do you want to see a magic fly?'

'No,' I said. But then I thought of Tal and changed my mind. I could keep James distracted while he sneaked back to the day room and out of trouble. 'Okay, yes.' We got out on the ground floor.

'Follow me,' he said.

We went to the kitchen. The stainless steel surfaces gleamed and the freezer hummed.

With his free hand, James filled a blue plastic beaker with water and dropped the fly in it. 'Watch!'

I watched the bluebottle struggle bravely for a few moments. Gradually it grew still.

'You're weird,' I said.

He fished it out and it lay on his finger –a wet, fuzzy blob. 'It's dead, right?' he asked, flicking it onto the table.

'Yeah. You just drowned it.'

'Give me a hair.'

'What?'

'A hair from your head,' James said impatiently, 'quick!'

I pulled a blonde hair out and gave it to him.

He tied it around the dead fly. Then he unhooked his keys, opened a cupboard door and brought out a tub of Saxo salt. 'See?' he said, and he sprinkled salt on the fly.

I cringed. 'Don't tell me you're going to eat it.'

'Just watch, Ava,' he said softly.

Time goes slowly when you're watching a dead bluebottle. But after a couple of minutes, it started to wave its legs.

'Hooray!' I cheered as it righted itself.

James picked up my strand of hair carefully, and a few moments later, the fly unfolded its wings and flew off the table – but not very far; with the hair tied around it, it whirled around our heads in circles, like a helicopter.

'See?' he said. 'It's a magic fly. Do you want a try?'

'No, don't worry,' I said, backing off, 'I'm good.' But it was a fantastic trick, I had to admit. 'How do you do that?'

He shrugged. 'I think the salt must dry it out or something.' He opened the window and let it go.

We watched it zigzagging out of sight and James shut the window.

'I've got to get back to work,' he said. 'The laundry man's coming at four. See ya.' He walked through the kitchen, keys jingling.

Sian Llewelyn was smoking outside, looking towards the oak trees. She turned as I reached the door and shook her brown hair away from her face.

'Oh, it's you.' She dropped her cigarette and twisted her foot on it.

She stared at me in the way adults do when they don't care if you like them or not. 'Your Nain's settling in nicely,' she said, kicking the squashed butt into the bushes.

'I know. But she's coming home soon.'

Sian Llewelyn narrowed her eyes, crushing her eyelashes so they looked like trapped spiders. 'I don't think so,' she said. 'I don't know where you got that idea.'

'But she told me she was!'

Sian laughed spitefully. 'She's senile. Old people say all sorts of things – believe me, I've heard it all.' She brushed her shiny hair from her face. 'This is her home now. She's got dementia, you know.'

I wanted to kick her. 'No she hasn't! She's just -'

'She's just what?' Sian prompted me, bending so close that I could feel drops of her spit on my face. 'Go on! Say it!'

The word PRETENDING flashed into my thoughts so brightly that I could see her reading the word in my mind. 'She's coming home!' I repeated instead and I stomped off, feeling angry and a little bit scared. I knew there was nothing wrong with Nain except for her feet and that horrible pink cardigan. I would ask Dad to let her come out as soon as possible. I would make him take her out.

As I marched down the drive I could feel her looking at me. I didn't look back.

My next job was to go to Idrys's old house, and once I'd gone through the gates I patted my right pocket for the list. It wasn't there, so I felt in the other one. Then I checked them all over again.

Noooo!

The fly wasn't James Dodd's only trick, I thought, feeling really annoyed with myself.

The list had disappeared.

Chapter Nine

Luckily, I'd memorised Idrys's old address, so I went straight from Whitehill to number six, Moreton Avenue, Idrys's old house.

A dog barked as the lady answered the door. She was eating toast in a pink dressing gown and holding a little girl who was sucking a pink dummy. The dog was like a very short black Alsatian, and it sniffed my feet.

'No sponsored walks,' she said.

'Okay.' I don't like walking, anyway. 'Gorgeous dog. What is he?'

'Alsatian-corgi cross.'

I started to pat him but he growled, so I put my hands in my pockets.

'What do you want?' the woman asked. She looked as if she was ready to slam the door on me.

'I just want to know – do you know what happened to the things that Idrys Jones left behind when he sold the house to you?'

She looked at me suspiciously. 'What's it got to do with you?'

'I just wondered, that's all.'

She raised her eyebrows, and took another bite of her toast.

'That's a funny thing to wonder about, if you ask me.'

'Did he leave any books behind, do you know?'

She started to look cross.

'Books? I know what he did leave behind - a mess, that's what he left. Stuffed animals, compasses, carved sticks and you should have seen the carpets – worn to threads - I had to have them ripped out in the end. I'd be ashamed of leaving a mess like that. We had to hire a skip – not a three quarters one either – a full size one. And that –' she pointed her crust at me – 'should give you an idea of the amount of rubbish that was in here.'

'So the books went in the skip, too?'

'He didn't have any books, I told you that.'

I didn't believe her.

'He was a teacher. Teachers always have books.'

'I don't care what he was, he didn't have any,' she said firmly. 'Anyway, what do you want to know about his books for?'

I think lying to James must have got me warmed up, because I said, 'My Nain lent him one, and now she wants it back.'

'She's left it a bit late, tell her. He must have got rid of it before he moved out.'

The dog was sniffing the step. She hooked him back inside with her leg and started to shut the door on me.

I was walking down the path when she opened the door again.

'Just a minute,' she said.

It was just like in a film where somebody remembers something very important at the last minute. I hurried back. 'Yes?' My voice came out all squeaky.

'He had a picture,' she said. 'It was the only decent thing in the house, and I've kept it because I like it.'

'Can I see it?' I glanced at the beige carpet. 'I'll take my shoes off.'

'I suppose so,' she said, and took me into the lounge. The dog followed us, with his nose on the backs of my knees.

The picture was in a gold frame, hanging above the fireplace.

It was of an old man in a cave, at night, his face lit by a candle, and someone was coming along a path towards him. It was gloomy. I wouldn't have kept it. But I had a good look at it anyway. There was a book in the picture but it didn't really help and it wasn't made out of flesh, it was purple.

The little girl started to wriggle and the woman put her down without taking her eyes off me. I think she thought I was going to steal it. 'Thanks,' I said finally. 'It's really nice.'

She walked me back to the door, and I sat on the bottom step to put my shoes on.

'Wasn't there even one book?' I asked her hopefully, in case she suddenly remembered it.

She shut the door on me.

As I walked back past the shops I saw that the chip shop, for once, was open and I bought a small chips with lots of salt and vinegar.

Coming out of the shop, I saw Tal walking towards me like a black shadow. His fair hair was limp and sweaty over one eye.

'What's the news?' he asked hopefully.

'No luck,' I said. 'The woman at his old house said he didn't leave any books.'

'So that's that.' Tal took a big, fat chip. 'I had to laugh,' he said, 'when James Dodd asked you for the list and you didn't give it to him. "You want my shopping list? You want to do it for me? You want to shop?"'

I was pleased with my quick thinking, too. 'Even if he'd taken the list,' I said casually, 'it wouldn't really matter, would it?'

Tal took another chip. 'I don't know. We shouldn't have written the name of the Book down, you know. Druids never write things down. We have to memorize everything.'

'Yes, but – it doesn't matter, though, does it?' I persisted.

'Just to be safe…' Tal took a cigarette lighter from his pocket. '…give it to me and I'll burn it.'

I offered him another chip. 'The thing is, James showed me the magic fly trick – you know the magic fly? And somehow – I mean, he brought it back from the dead, so it was quite interesting and I thought it would give you time to get back to the day room without anyone knowing, and then when I got to the gate I felt in my pocket and – ' I shrugged with one hand. 'It had gone.'

'You lost it?'

'No! I didn't lose it! James must have taken it!'

'Great,' Tal said, stuffing the lighter back into his pocket.

'But we only had two places on the list and the Book isn't in either of them.'

'But now,' Tal said, 'James knows about the Book.'

That was true. 'So? He's not a druid, is he?'

'He's not a druid, no,' Tal said as we crossed the road. 'But he wishes he was. His Dad's the archdruid. He sent him to Idrys for a couple of years when he was a little kid but Idrys said he wasn't right for it. He was too wild and it didn't work out so he took me on instead.'

At that moment, I felt really sorry for James Dodd. I knew what it was like to fail when you were a little kid, too. I had to go for an interview for a pre-prep school when I was four, and as Mum and Dad sat down with the headmaster, Mr Wigglesworth, I hid under his desk and refused to come out. I remember staring at his shiny black shoes and wanting to pull them off his feet and throw them in the fire.

But the point is, I didn't get into that first school and my parents were disappointed in me and that was the reason why. 'I don't think James would care about a book, anyway,' I said. 'He wears camouflage and all that and he likes terrorists. He probably thought I was writing something about him, and that's why I was hiding it.'

'He'd like that,' Tal said, and he shuffled off home in a bad mood.

Chapter Ten

On Tuesday afternoon it was Idrys's funeral.

'I'm going to Chester for a black dress,' Caroline said that morning.

'You can't wear black,' Dad said scornfully, frowning at us from the Sports pages. 'Not for a druid's funeral.'

Caroline and I looked at each other.

'There's a dress code?' Caroline asked.

'No. There's no dress code except you don't wear black. He's not dead, is he? He's just passed on.'

Caroline and I looked at him, baffled.

Dad added, 'And you have to take a gift.'

Caroline poured herself another coffee. 'A gift? For who?'

'For Idrys,' Dad said. 'For, you know…' he jerked his thumb towards the ceiling.

Caroline and I looked up nervously – I don't know what we expected to see.

'For him to use up there,' Dad said.

Caroline glanced at me, eyebrows high. Her eyes were very green and I knew she was thinking – Is he mad?

'What kind of gift shall we get?' I asked him.

'I've got him a mobile phone,' Dad said smugly, folding his paper up. 'A Motorola. Hello, Moto!'

My dad is the most boringly normal person there is, so it gave me a funny feeling to hear he'd been buying a phone for a dead guy.

'A phone?' Caroline said. 'You bought him a phone?'

'What if he rings us?'

Dad gave us a look.

'Where's he going to get it topped up?' I asked. 'Is – you know – heaven the same as here?' I don't know why, but the thought of shops in heaven was a bit disappointing. Not that I've got anything against them. Except that in the one by our school, they only let you in two at a time, and by the time you get to the counter, lunchtime is over.

'Or did you buy it with a contract?' Caroline asked slowly.

'What? No!' Dad said.

'If you had, we'd be able to check the bill and see who he calls,' I pointed out.

'So what do you want me to get him,' Caroline said sarcastically. 'Sat nav? So he can find his way back?'

'That's a bit over the top,' Dad said in a dignified way, 'seeing as you didn't even know him. He liked Terry's Chocolate Orange.'

We didn't go shopping after all. You can get those in the Nisa shop.

Idrys's funeral didn't take place in a church. It took place on a grassy hill, by a noisy stream, in the middle of some small standing stones that looked like a mini Stonehenge.

It was more like a picnic than a funeral.

The day was sunny, the sky was deep blue and the grass was short and springy. Caroline's high heels sank into the soft ground so every time I looked at her she was standing at an angle. Dad was right; no-one wore black, and there were a lot of druids standing by the coffin wearing long robes, some white, some blue and some green.

Caroline pushed her Christian Dior sunglasses to the top of her head and leant against a tall stone. She was wearing a red and white dress. 'Open coffin,' she said, glancing towards the place where the druids were standing. 'I'd kill for a cigarette. Go and see if someone's put some in there.'

'I'm not stealing from a dead man,' I said indignantly. I stomped over to see Tal. He was wearing white robes and I could see his trainers underneath. I'd never seen him wearing anything white before. He looked as if he was an angel in a school play. He was talking to a tall man in a white suit.

When he saw me, he waved.

'Hi!' I said. 'We bought him a Terry's Chocolate Orange.'

'Go and give it to him,' he said, and I went over to Idrys's coffin feeling a bit nervous. The coffin was like a huge wicker basket, lying on top of a flat stone. I had never seen a dead person before and I worried that I would feel sad and cry. But Idrys looked all right; a bit pale, maybe, but not scary at all. He was wearing white robes and holding a huge

96

bunch of mistletoe and he was surrounded by his presents. There were bottles of wine, a Welsh Monopoly board, chocolate oranges (five, but if there weren't newsagents in heaven I suppose they'd have to last), tins of food and an iPod; and now he had a Motorola mobile, too.

I don't know why, but seeing him with all those presents made me feel better.

As I put the chocolate orange into the coffin, Sian Llewelyn came to stand on the other side. She was dressed in blue.

'You again,' she said coldly, tucking an envelope into the coffin.

She made it sound as if I was stalking her or something.

'Yes,' I said. I wondered what was in the envelope. Money, hopefully, but maybe it was a gift voucher. How would you know which shops were in heaven?

A breeze blew over us and billowed under Sian's blue robes.

I imagined her taking off like a balloon and floating down the mountain. Wishful thinking.

'Poor Idrys,' she said over her shoulder as she moved away. 'If only you'd caught up with him that day.'

A tall, thin man came to look at Idrys, too. He was wearing a cream suit and a brown shirt. He had very black hair in a quiff quite low down his forehead which made him look like an Elvis impersonator. As he scratched his forehead, his fingers completely disappeared underneath his hair. Argh!!!

He saw me looking at him.

'Excuse the wig,' he apologized, and adjusted it.

'Okay,' I said, deeply embarrassed.

He looked into the coffin. 'Hello, Idrys, old mate,' he said. 'Lazing around as usual.' Then he looked at me again. 'My little joke. He was a good friend of mine. You're Michael's daughter, aren't you? I remember your dad when he was this high –' he held his hand up – 'and he used to come into my bookshop looking for Sci-fi. Are you a reader?'

'Yes.'

'What's your genre?'

'I like Anthony Horowitz,' I said, 'but if I'm bored I read anything.'

'Always a pleasure to meet a book-lover,' he said, and he held out his hand and gave me his card. 'I give favoured clients a discount. Gwilliam Johnson. For all your book solutions.'

'Ava Jones.' I shook his hand over Idrys's body and tried not to look at Gwilliam's wig.

Suddenly a bugle blew.

'That's the archdruid,' Gwilliam said. 'Stand to attention!'

Everyone fell quiet as the bugle notes died away. The archdruid was very tall. He was wearing white, with a gold metal cape, and he was the loudest man I'd ever heard. He stood in the centre of the standing stones with his arms outstretched.

'WE ARE GATHERED HERE, FRIENDS, DRUIDS FROM THE HENGE OF BRÂN AND DRUIDS FROM THE SONS OF LLYR, UNITED UNDER THE PROTECTION OF BLESSED BRÂN WHO BROUGHT CHRISTIANITY TO THIS ISLAND, TO WAVE OFF OUR OLD FRIEND IDRYS INTO THE OTHERWORLD.'

His voice seemed to travel across the mountains, and even the clouds moved more quickly as he spoke.

'IDRYS WAS A MAN OF MANY ASPECTS. THERE WAS IDRYS THE

TEACHER, AND IDRYS THE PHILOSOPHER, IDRYS THE LOYAL, IDRYS THE SAGE AND,' he paused, looking humorously at us from under his eyebrows, 'IDRYS THE FORGETFUL.'

I looked at Tal and he grinned at me.

'BUT WHAT IDRYS DIDN'T FORGET WAS HIS PLACE IN THIS WORLD. HE DIDN'T FORGET TO RESPECT IT AND HE DIDN'T FORGET THE NEED TO PROTECT IT, IN THE NAME OF BLESSED BRÂN.'

Around us, the druids agreed in a rumble like distant thunder.

'YES INDEED,' the archdruid said. 'IT NEEDS PROTECTING. IT NEEDS PROTECTING FROM THOSE WHO SEEK POWER -' He stopped abruptly and looked at someone moving behind the stone circle.

Everyone else looked, too.

It was James Dodd.

He was wearing his camouflage gear and sneaking around from one stone to the next like a commando. He didn't seem to care that we were watching him. He had something in a carrier bag and it looked heavy.

The archdruid narrowed his eyes as he stared at James, giving him evil looks. Only a father could look at a kid as fiercely as that.

'IT NEEDS PROTECTING,' he bellowed at him, 'FROM THOSE WHO REJOICE IN DESTRUCTION.'

James Dodd ignored him and came over to the coffin with his mysteriously heavy package. He took some boxes out of the bag and piled them up by Idrys's feet.

'AND TO THIS END, OUR OLD FRIEND IDRYS SHOWED HIS GRAND CONTEMPT FOR MORTAL LOT BY COMING TO THESE MOUNTAINS TO REST. HIS SPIRIT NOW HAS A BODY ELSEWHERE, SAFE WITH THE SECRET AND THE SUBLIME. MY FRIENDS, IT IS GIVEN TO US DRUIDS TO KNOW THE WISDOM OF NATURE, THE SIZE AND SHAPE OF THE UNIVERSE, AND TO KNOW THAT DEATH IS NOT THE END, BUT THE MIDPOINT OF LIFE.'

The boxes said Express on them. Twelve gauge. I didn't have time to look any closer, because the druids were lining up in two rows and Tal was holding a huge sword in a dark sheath– I don't know where he got it from.

The archdruid pulled it part way out the sheath and shouted: 'IS THERE PEACE?

'Not with a voice like that, there isn't,' James muttered, glancing at me through his dark eyelashes.

I giggled, but everyone else shouted, 'PEACE!'

And then the archdruid repeated it.

After the third time, he handed the sheathed sword back to Tal.

The druids gathered round the coffin and picked it up and carried it from the standing stones to a shiny black hearse that had just drawn up on the narrow road, with Tal leading the way. We watched the druids drift past us as they followed the hearse down the road and back to the village.

'Now what's going to happen?' I asked James.

'They're going to bury him in the Church cemetery. What did you think they were going to do?'

I thought about it, and brushed my hair out of my eyes. 'I don't know.' But I did know. I thought they would leave him high up on the mountains to be eaten by ravens, until the birds were red with blood. Shivering, I looked for Dad. He was holding Caroline's hand and Caroline was barefoot, because her shoes had mud and grass stuck on the heels, so I stayed with James Dodd as we walked back down the hill. 'What gift did you give him?' I asked curiously.

'It's private,' he said.

'Is it? I gave him a Terry's Chocolate Orange.'

James grinned suddenly and flicked his black hair out of his eyes. 'You only told me so that I'd tell you what I gave him.'

'Yeah,' I said. 'I know.'

'I gave him shotgun cartridges,' he said, looking at me though his dark eyelashes. 'I blew up Offa's Dyke once with a shotgun cartridge. I wedged it into the dyke and shot the cap with an air pistol. BOOOM!'

I stared at him. 'Why would he need shotgun cartridges in heaven?'

'Why would he need a chocolate orange?'

I shrugged. 'Don't ask me,' I said. 'I don't know anything about druids.'

I kicked some stones, but they turned out to be sheep droppings. Yuk.

We came to the track that led to the road through the village.

'This lot aren't like the old druids,' James said, stopping to point at a falcon with his finger and pulling an imaginary trigger. 'Pow!' He turned to look at me. 'The old druids cut animals open and read the future in their guts and blood-splatter. Honest. It's called divination. Old druids were into human sacrifices and things like that.'

'Really?' I shivered, even though I only half-believed him. 'How do you know that?'

'Because my dad told me. He knows everything about that sort of thing but it's wasted on him really. He's into conservation and stuff.' He looked at me through his black fringe. 'It will be different when we find the Head of Brân.'

I felt as if I'd had an electric shock. 'The Head of Brân?'

'Yeah…Idrys used to ramble on about what amazing powers it has. So Sian and I are going to find it and try it out for ourselves. See what we can do with it.'

I tried to act casual, although my voice had gone squeaky. 'Do you know where it is?'

'Not yet. We're still looking.'

I glanced at James with relief. 'So that's that,' I said hopefully, trying to bluff. 'I guess it will never be found now that Idrys's dead.'

James had a bit of a smile on his face. 'Can't it?' He turned to look at me. Not just a glance, but a real look. 'Idrys isn't the only one who was bad at keeping secrets, Ava Jones,' he said. He gave me a folded piece of paper. 'You dropped this in the kitchen the other day.'

I knew what it was. The list!

'That list is private,' I said, watching people standing around the hole in the ground that was Idrys's grave.

As I turned to look at James, his eyes were as blue as the blue lagoon.

He grinned. 'You should have taken better care of it, then,' he said.

Chapter Eleven

That night I tried to work out what we should do next. We couldn't find the Head until we found the book. And if we couldn't find the book, we were stuck.

I started to get undressed and I was folding up my jeans when I found Gwilliam Johnson's card in my pocket. I sat on the bed and studied it. It said:

GWILLIAM JOHNSON BOOKS
For All Your Book Needs
Rare and Secondhand
Bought and Sold
Will Collect
Many Subjects Covered
We are always willing to buy large and small collections
www.gwilliamjohnsonbooks.co.uk

I read it all over again thoughtfully and started to get excited. Gwilliam was Idrys's friend. He collected rare books. Maybe Idrys had given him the Druid's Book! The more I thought about it, the more logical it was.

I put my jeans back on again and hurried downstairs.

Dad was sitting by the table eating crisps and finishing off a glass of red wine. He had crumbs on his shirt. 'I thought you'd gone to bed,' he said.

'I have to see Tal urgently. Please? I won't be a minute.'

'At this time of night? He's got work in the morning.'

'Pleeeeease?'

Dad looked at the clock. 'Tell you what,' he said, 'I could do with stretching my legs. We'll walk round there and if he's up you can have a quick word. A Quick Word, do you hear?'

'Yes!'

He popped into the parlour to tell Caroline we were going to 'stretch our legs', and we walked through the cool night to Tal's house. We could see the lights glowing in the darkness, warm and welcoming.

Dad waited by the gate, whistling.

Tal's dad answered the door. It was the man in the white suit. He looked like a film star, or at least, a newsreader.

I was too surprised to speak, but he said,

'Hello, kiddo. Come on in.' He sounded like a newsreader, too.

Tal was in the dining room with his mother, icing cupcakes. She smiled at me and her teeth were amazingly white. She looked like a film star, too.

He took me into the kitchen and I showed him the business card that Gwilliam had given me. 'This is where the Book is,' I whispered. 'I'll bet you anything.'

Tal frowned and leant against the cooker. 'You think Idrys gave it to Gwilliam Johnson?'

'Why not? He collects rare books! Look!' I showed him the card again.

He read it quickly and handed it back. 'I dunno,' he said. 'Idrys said I knew where the book was, but I didn't for a minute think it was Gwilliam's shop.'

'You didn't think it was anywhere,' I argued. 'You didn't even think there was a book.'

'I know,' he agreed and scratched his chest.

If it had been Rosie, she would have screamed, and I would have screamed, and we'd have jumped up and down with excitement. Instead I had Tal, looking doubtful. 'I got out of bed for this,' I protested. 'Listen, tomorrow we're going to the shop to see him. What time will you finish at Whitehill?'

'Five.'

'I'll meet you at Gwilliam's. Okay? Like about ten past?'

'Okay.'

'Okay.' It was like being on a secret mission. I said goodbye to his parents and joined Dad who was lurking by the gate. Compared with Tal's dad, he looked boringly normal.

'Didn't you ever think of getting a white suit?' I asked him as we walked back in the dark.

'Of course not. It's impractical. Your mother would never have allowed it.'

'But you could have one now she's gone,' I said. It was a trap. I waited for him to say that one day, she'd be back. But he didn't.

The following afternoon at ten past five, I met Tal at the bookshop. It was bright and modern, with a children's corner which had two red beanbags on the floor. Gwilliam Johnson was sitting behind the counter, wearing a white polo shirt and drinking a cup of coffee when we went in. The cup had BOOKWORM written on it in red letters. His wig was on straight, but I couldn't help noticing it all the same.

'Oh, hullo, hullo again,' he said as we came in. He took off his glasses and wiped them. 'Fine assembly we had for Idrys's funeral yesterday, wasn't it?'

'Yeah,' Tal and I said together.

'The Anthony Horowitz's, young lady, are in that section on the right.'

'Well actually –' I could see the old books lined up in a locked, glass fronted case behind the counter. The gold lettering glowed warmly against dark leather, but I was looking for something sort of pink and skin-like. Yuk.

Gwilliam saw me looking. 'You have an interest in old books, do you?'

'Yes, and you've got a lot of them,' I said, trying to sound impressed.

'Ah,' he said, 'I'm very much a collector.'

'Have you ever heard of such a thing as a book being bound in human skin?' I asked brightly.

Gwilliam Johnson's face lit up. 'Good gracious me,' he said. 'You're interested in anthropodermic bibliopegy?'

Was I??? 'Yes,' I said firmly. And then I had some inspiration. 'It's for a school project.'

'Which school do you go to?'

'Devonshire House. It's in London.'

He looked relieved. 'For a moment I thought I was going to be swamped with children,' he said. 'Every time the schools set a project, I get swamped; absolutely swamped. Now, I know what's set this off. I bet you've been reading about *A True and Perfect Relation of the Whole Proceedings against the Late and Most Barbarous Traitors, Garnet, a Jesuit and His Confederates.* Am I right?'

I nodded, trying to look as if I knew what he was talking about. 'And other similar books,' I said.

'Well of course,' he said happily, 'and there are many. Anthropodermic bibliopegy really wasn't very unusual, and in the seventeen and eighteen hundreds it was quite common to bind murder trial transcripts with the criminals' skin.'

'Eew.'

He looked at us over his glasses. 'Might be a practice the government would think of resurrecting. Recycling in its finest form. Nothing wasted. It would be enough to put you off crime, wouldn't it,' he chuckled.

'Definitely,' I agreed.

'The interesting aspect of *A True and Perfect* is the appearance of Garnet's face on the cover.'

'They used the skin from his *face*?'

'No no no no no! Too uneven – and of course, full of holes.'

'Holes?'

'Eyes and nostrils.'

I felt sick.

'No,' he went on, 'what you need is a good sized piece of skin for the cover, such as the skin from a person's back. The pores give it a nice texture. It can be buffed, like leather. It's durable, too and a useful alternative to calfskin.' He gave a small smile.

'So if it was skin from his back, how did his face appear on the cover of the book?'

Gwilliam Johnson smiled. 'It appeared like magic, young lady, screaming his innocence; like a photograph developing before the eyes. And a bloodstain on a strand of straw at the place of his execution also shaped itself into an image of his guiltless face.'

It was the creepiest thing I had ever heard. 'Where is the bloodstained straw now?'

'Rotted away.'

I'd gone goose-pimply all over. 'So what had Garnet the Jesuit done? Did he kill someone?'

'He was accused of being involved in the Gunpowder Plot.' Gwilliam Johnson leant towards me. 'Remember, Remember, the Fifth of November.' He shifted his wig. 'Scholars think he was innocent, you know. But he was powerless, of course, to fight back.'

I was glad that the sun was shining in through the window.

As it was, I was going to have nightmares; I knew it.

Tal had been standing quietly next to me, but he suddenly came to life. 'Idrys had a book like that. An example of anthropodermic bibliopegy. We thought he might have given it to you.'

I was astonished that he'd remembered the anthropo-thingy word.

Gwilliam raised his eyebrows so high they almost disappeared under the wig. 'Idrys had a book?' He sounded shocked. 'What is the content?'

'Druidic history,' Tal said.

'Druids…? No. Impossible. He didn't mention it me.' He rubbed his fingers over his thin lips. 'I find that surprising considering the length of our friendship, especially during his latter days in Whitehill. And to be honest…' he looked at Tal, 'I suppose I find it…a little unusual in the circumstances. But if this book does indeed exist, I would be most interested to see it. Druidic history, you say?'

Tal nodded.

'Where did he get hold of it?'

'I don't know. That's the funny thing - he only told me about it the day he died.'

'Well,' Gwilliam said, rubbing his hands, 'when you find it, bring it to me;

bring it to me and I'll have a look at it.' He extended his neck and looked at us piercingly over the counter as though he was trying to read our minds. Then he said,

'I can tell you something, there are a lot of book collectors that would pay a great deal of money to see that. Including, I may tell you, my good self. Yes indeed. A great deal of money.'

'Really?' I asked, imagining how much a great deal of money was. Thousands, probably. 'This book; what would the cover look like? Pink?'

Gwilliam covered his smile with his fingers. 'Not pink. Human leather,' he said delicately, 'is a sort of golden brown. It may be tooled and decorated, possibly, given the subject.' He handed Tal a business card from a little holder on the counter. 'Give me a call if you find it. And you, young lady – good luck with your project. If you'd like to give me your contact details, I'll get in touch with you with anything else I come across that might be of interest.' He pushed a black leather comments book towards me and handed me a pen.

He was so nice and helpful that I felt bad for lying to him. I wrote my home address and phone number down as neatly as I could. 'Thank you,' I said in a small voice.

'The pleasure is all mine,' he said, and he followed us to the door and slid the sign to CLOSED. I looked at my watch.

It was five-thirty.

'Are you going to the church quiz tonight?' Tal asked as we reached the playground at the back of Nain's house.

'I don't know anything about it. Are you?'

'Yes.' He jumped on a swing. 'You can come with us if you like. I'm going with my parents. There'll be food, and there's prizes,' he said, swinging higher.

I liked the sound of that. 'What prizes?'

'Money - a hundred pounds for the winning team. But you have to pay six quid to enter.'

'A hundred pounds each?'

'No, to share. But there will only be four of us on our table.'

'Twenty-five pounds each, if we win? Are your parents good at quizzes?'

Tal grinned. 'No. But I am.'

I didn't know if it was true or not. But it wasn't as if I had anything else to do. And twenty-five pounds – I liked the sound of that. 'I'll ask,' I said.

When I got back to Nain's house, they were in the garden. Caroline was sitting on a patterned sun lounger, sunbathing. You could see her a mile off – she was as white as a ghost, covered with factor 75.

Dad was sitting in the shade. He liked the sound of the quiz. 'We could come. I'm quite good at quizzes,' he said.

It's true he does do a lot of shouting during Mastermind. I sat on the lawn and started to work out what a hundred divided by six was. Sixteen pounds something. It wasn't as if Dad needed the money. 'Did I say it's in the church?'

'In the church, is it?' He flicked a fly off his arm and looked thoughtful. 'It won't be all religious questions, will it? Out of the Bible?'

'Probably, as it's a church quiz.'

'What do you think, Caroline? Shall we go?'

She took her sunglasses off and by the way she looked at him I could see it was a No.

Dad patted me on the back. 'Next time,' he promised. 'Anyway, you'll probably have more fun without us.'

As I found out when I got there at seven o'clock that evening, it wasn't in the church, it was in the church hall. There were lots of tables with tablecloths on, and white candles in jars. Men were unloading wine from cool boxes and women were hurrying in with steaming Pyrex dishes and oven gloves, shouting warnings.

Tal waved me over.

'Do you like couscous, Ava?' his mother asked, taking the foil of a brown dish.

'I'll eat anything,' I said truthfully.

'Samosas?'

'Yes.' I looked at Fred in his white suit.

'Help yourself, kiddo,' he said.

I put the plates out, and forks for each of us - my friends' parents really like me for doing that sort of thing. They wish that they had daughters like me. I don't do it in my own house of course. That would be weird and unnatural.

Fred Evans asked, 'Your Nain's at Whitehill, isn't she? Where Idrys used to be?'

'Yes.'

'Shame about Idrys. He was a wise man. I'm writing an elegy about him.'

I nodded politely. On the other tables I recognised Gwilliam Johnson and the nurse from Whitehill. I noticed that we were getting some looks from the other people. They were not disapproving looks exactly, more like the thoughtful looks you give each other when you're lining up in the pool before the starter gun goes off. I hoped they didn't think I was going to know all the answers.

At the front of the hall was a big flip chart, divided into sections. We were Team Five. I looked at the lists of subjects. History, Geography, Science, General Knowledge, Sport, Entertainment and Food and I started feeling nervous.

'Here, Ava,' his mother said, offering me the brown dish. 'Help yourself.'

I did, and afterwards I passed Tal the brown dish just as the tall thin woman tapped the microphone. It gave a high-pitched scream.

'Are you all ready? Question number one. Which is the tallest cathedral in the British Isles?'

I stared at her blankly. How would I know? Westminster? That wasn't very tall, was it? Winchester? I'd never been to Winchester. What, are you supposed to go to cathedrals with a tape measure now?

It didn't matter, because luckily, Tal was already scribbling an answer down.

His parents settled back on the grey plastic chairs and started eating. I started to eat too, to give myself an excuse for not answering, but it didn't matter, because as soon as the tall thin woman read next the question, Tal wrote down the answer. He reminded me of Rosie in exams.

I looked at him in surprise. We had bright kids in our school so it wasn't as if I'd never seen one before, but I hadn't thought of Tal as bright. I just thought he knew a few things about birds. But then I remembered some of the things he'd talked about, like moral philosophy and natural philosophy, and how he'd remembered that word to describe books bound in human skin; yeah. The anthropo word. That was bright. Idrys was right; Tal had already learned a lot.

Occasionally someone on another table would say an answer too loudly and get shushed by all the others, but it didn't matter to us. Tal wasn't even listening. He didn't need to. He could have taken a table by himself and been his own quiz team and kept the hundred pounds all for himself for all the help we were.

The couscous was really nice and the samosas were still warm from the oven, crispy on the outside and spicy on the inside. Jill encouraged me to be greedy. 'Will you have another?' she asked every time I stopped for a rest.

After fifteen questions, we had to swap papers with another table, to be marked. When ours came back, it had 15 with a circle around it. Top marks!

'How do you know so much?' I asked Tal before the next round started.

Tal looked surprised that I'd asked, and then he chewed his thumbnail as though he was embarrassed. 'Because of my memory,' he said after a moment. 'I've been memorising things all my life, haven't I?'

'Why? For quizzes?'

'No, to be a druid.' He picked up a samosa and dipped it into a minty dip. 'Druids don't write things down because the written word is sacred. We learn everything by heart. It takes years to learn it all.'

'Oh, yes. You told me that. And can you remember everything you learn?'

'Yeah; I remember everything I learn, and everything I say. And everything everyone else does and says.' He stuffed the whole samosa into his mouth.

'Really?' I couldn't believe he hadn't mentioned this before now. It sounded a great trick. 'What were the first words I said?'

'"You have to ring the buzzer and they'll open it".'

'Cool!' I was amazed at how long ago that day seemed, when Idrys gave him a Chinese burn and I'd felt sorry for him. 'And can you – ' but I stopped because the questions started on History. Yuk!

You know University Challenge? You know how there's always one person in a team who doesn't answer anything for ages?

Well, at the Church Quiz, that was me. There wasn't a single question that I knew the answer to. Sometimes I didn't even understand the question, but I tried my best to look excited or thoughtful and I got quite good at it.

But then, on the last subject, Food, I totally redeemed myself.

The third question was: what is the singular of scampi?

And I knew it! Hooray! 'Scampo,' I whispered loudly. I felt really pleased. I felt as if I was on TV and I could hear the cheers.

I went into a daydream. Tal could make money with a memory like that. He could be on Who Wants to Be a Millionaire. He could be rich!

And then I started thinking of Idrys. If everything he knew was learned by heart and all his knowledge had been in his memory, it must have been a terrible thing when his memory went. He wouldn't even be able to look anything up that he needed to know; druids never wrote in books because the written word was sacred.

And I realised that was the reason he didn't leave any books behind. The woman in his old house was right! Even though he was a teacher, he didn't have any books and I knew why, now. He didn't need them. He was a druid, and he didn't have books because the written word was...

Sacred.

A shiver went through me. Just a minute!

I put my samosa down.

It didn't make sense - if druids didn't have books, what exactly was Idrys talking about?

I looked at Tal. His face was shining and his fair hair was flopping to one side. He was still writing on the sheet. He was amazing - he was like a human reference book, covered in skin.

I felt as if an electric shock was running through me; I could feel the hairs standing up on my arms. He was a human reference book! I grabbed his arm. 'Tal! Tal! I know where the Druid's Book is!' I said.

He scratched his chin with the pen and looked startled. 'What? Where is it?'

'Tal,' I said, poking him in the chest, 'it's YOU!'

Chapter Twelve

Tal, alias the Druid's Book, stared at me.

I grinned proudly. 'Go on,' I said excitedly, 'tell me I'm a genius. Nain was right! You can never judge a book by its cover!'

Just then we had to go up for the prize money of twenty-five pounds each and a box of Celebrations, and everyone in the church hall clapped. As we went back our table, he told his parents that he was leaving.

'Coming?' he asked me, jabbing me with his elbow.

We stood up to leave. I thanked his mother for the food and she wrapped some cupcakes in foil in case we felt hungry on the walk home.

It was dark as we left the church hall.

Tal turned the corner into the gloomy church yard. Reluctantly, I followed him. I don't like graveyards, especially at night. 'So - where's the Head?' I asked him.

'I've told you, I don't know where it is,' Tal said moodily, going to Idrys's grave.

We walked through the long black shadows of grave stones on the silvery grass and Tal crouched by the dark mound of earth that buried Idrys. 'I wish he'd stayed,' he said. 'He shouldn't have left me. I still have seven years' worth of stuff to learn. I don't know any of the important things. I'm not even good at seeing the future.'

The cellophane on the flowers whispered and rustled in the breeze.

'But you know the history of the druids, right? I mean, you're the Book! And if you're the Book and you've got an amazing memory, then you must know where the Head is. And that's all that matters.'

Cars hummed softly along the road and a dog barked at its own echo.

Tal said, 'You think it's simple, don't you?' He flicked his fair hair out of his eyes and looked up at me. 'But it isn't at all. I mean,' he said, 'what did you do this time last month?'

'Well,' I said, thinking about it, 'this time last month I was probably watching TV. Or on Facebook. Hang on - Rosie had a sleepover after the exams finished. I don't think that was a month ago, though. Ooh, just a minute - we broke up on - '

'Yeah, exactly,' Tal interrupted. 'Remembering's not like Googling where you can click onto a subject and find what you want just like that. It's more like searching through boxes and boxes of pointless stuff until you come across the valuable bits.'

And suddenly, I understood.

It was different when we thought there was a proper book to flick through, a book which would have a Head-finding chapter with instructions and that kind of thing. But I didn't have a clue how you went about flicking through a person. 'That's okay,' I said, 'just go through everything until you find it.'

'That means I have to start reciting it all from the beginning, from the very beginning, just as I learnt it.' Tal pulled a silver strand of grass from the graveside and chewed it. 'It takes seventy hours and forty minutes to read the Bible aloud,' he said, spitting it out. 'To recite the druids' history could take weeks.'

'Really?' I hadn't realized that. I get bored during lessons and they only last for forty minutes. But this wasn't school; this was important. 'So who cares?' I said recklessly. 'I've got the whole of the summer holidays to listen to you, and I'm good at ignoring the pointless stuff, so you don't have to worry about that.'

Tal poked me with his elbow. 'Hah! You'll fall asleep,' he said.

I poked him back. 'It can't be that boring, can it? If it's a story about a skull that can get you things, I'm interested,' I said, convincing myself. 'Go on, check me out.' The church clock struck, and I counted the bongs. Eleven o'clock! We started walking across the grass to the lych gate and our shadows slid out from underneath us, slithering over headstones.

Tal took a deep breath and then he said in a quiet voice, 'One. Three men who received the strength of Adam; Hercules the Strong, Hector the Strong and Adam the Strong.'

I opened my box of Celebrations and picked one out in the dark. I couldn't see what it was. Mmmm...

'All three were as strong as Adam himself. Two: Three men who received the beauty of Adam: Absalom, son of

128

David; Jason, son of Aeson; Paris, son of Priam. All three were as beautiful as Adam himself.'

Coming out through the dim lych gate into the glowing street was like being in another world.

People were walking home from the quiz, talking and laughing and calling goodnight from their brightly-lit doorways.

'Three,' Tal said as we reached my street corner. 'Three men who received the wisdom of Adam: Cato the Old, Bede, and Siblo the Wise. They were as wise as Adam himself.'

I was going home with my Celebrations, twenty-five pounds and the Druid's Book, audio version. I was happy.

'Are you still listening?'

'What? Oh, of course I am!'

He was right about one thing, I thought. It might take a long time.

Chapter Thirteen

The following morning the sun was shining through the skylight and I thought about my winnings and Tal reciting the opening lines of the Druid's Book.

As I went downstairs in Nain's dressing gown, I could hear Dad talking to Caroline about getting back to the office. As I opened the door, they both looked at me.

'Now, Ava,' Dad said seriously, hugging his coffee mug.

'What? What have I done?' I hadn't even sat down!

'Nain wants to come home.'

'Oh!' I said, suddenly feeling relieved. 'Great! At last!'

Dad ran his thumb around the rim of the mug. 'Sian Llewelyn's not convinced. But the doctor's checked Mam's mental state and she knows what year it is, who the Prime Minister is, and she can count from a hundred, backwards, subtracting sevens, which is more than I can do.'

I hoped he was joking. Caroline looked up and poured me a coffee.

'He says she's sharp as a knife,' Dad went on proudly, 'and that's good enough for me. I know my mother better than Sian Llewelyn does and as far as I'm concerned, if she says she's ready to come home, then she's ready.'

'I agree,' I said with relief.

'Yes, well, the point is, even though Nain's coming home, she's still not a hundred per cent. She will need someone to help with the shopping and cleaning. And I have to get back to work.'

I never thought I'd ever volunteer to clean, but I said quickly, 'I'll do it for her! I like shopping and cleaning.'

Dad looked doubtful. 'Ava, it wouldn't be your usual kind of holiday, you know.'

'I don't mind!'

'She won't be able to take you on jaunts, or anything like that.'

'That's okay. I don't care. I'll stay with her for the whole of the summer holidays if you like.'

Dad looked at Caroline. He looked worried, surprised and pleased, in that order.

'See?' Caroline said.

Dad nodded. This was a big deal, because usually he doesn't trust me to do anything, never mind something important.

In my mind I punched the air, feeling happy at how things had worked out. I could stay here all summer!

If it took seventy hours and forty minutes to read the Bible, we might need the whole summer, bearing in mind Tal was still on Adam.

I wasn't sure where Brân came in druid history, but I had a feeling he was a long time after that. I imagined sitting around in the evening on Nain's sofas, drinking Red Bull, eating Pringles and listening to him.

'Well,' Dad said with a relieved smile, 'that's settled that! I'll put some waffles on and then I'll call Whitehill.'

Suddenly the doorbell rang and we all looked at each other.

'Who's that?' Dad asked me.

I hate it when he says that. As if I can see through walls.

No-one moved, so I sighed, put my coffee down and went to answer it.

I was surprised to see it was Gwilliam Johnson from the bookshop. He had on a new curly brown wig. He was cheerfully rubbing his hands and he looked as though he had been up for hours.

I hate people who are really cheerful in the mornings.

'Ah!' he said, 'Just the girl I wanted to see! Did you enjoy yourself last night?'

I nodded, remembering my winnings.

Dad came up behind me to see who it was. He was still wearing his dressing gown too. Suddenly I had a horrible feeling that Gwilliam Johnson was going to mention the fake homework project in front of Dad. If he did, I knew what would happen. Dad would keep on at me until I did it. Can you imagine having to do homework that didn't really exist? It's bad enough doing genuine homework.

'Hello, Gwilliam,' Dad said.

'Hello, Michael!' Gwilliam smiled at him.

Just then I could smell burning waffles.

'Michaaaael!!!' Caroline shouted as smoke drifted through the dining room.

'Excuse me,' Dad said, and dashed to the kitchen.

'About this druid book,' Gwilliam said to me softly, rubbing his hands again. 'I'd like to offer my services and expertise in helping you search for it.'

I could hear Dad yelping - juggling hot waffles, at a guess.

'It's okay,' I said to Gwilliam, 'that's all sorted out now. We've found it.'

'You have?' He seemed surprised, but it could have been from the swear words Dad was using. 'May I see it?'

'It's not actually –' I was going to say it wasn't actually a book, but he interrupted me.

'I will pay you for a peek, Ava. Just a little peek,' he said softly.

I liked the sound of that. 'Really?' I imagined being Tal's agent and letting people peek at him for money. I could call him Memory Man - Mr. Mysterio Memory Man. We'd both be rich! 'How much?' I asked, out of curiosity.

'I'd like to see it first, just to see what I'm getting.'

'Ava!' Dad yelled.

'I'd better go. My father's cooking breakfast,' I said, expecting Dad to come back to chat to Gwilliam at any second, 'and then we're going to bring Nain home.'

Gwilliam put his foot in the door and stared at me, stroking his tie. 'That book is valuable and I want to see it. More importantly,' he added sternly, 'you would do well to remember that it's not your property. Finders isn't keepers in the eyes of the law.'

I heard the lid of the pedal bin clanking. 'Okay,' I said, because Dad was coming through the dining room, 'I'll remember that.'

He gave a bow, and his wig slid over his eyebrows.

I shut the door just in time.

Dad came up behind me. 'So,' he said, 'what did he want?'

'Tal and I went to his shop to look for a book, but now we've found it by ourselves.' I went into the dining room and glanced out of the window at the garden. Little brown sparrows were taking it in turns to fly from the kitchen roof to the laurel bush.

'I read a book, once,' Caroline said, sipping her coffee.

'What was it like?'

'Oh - it was sort of rectangular,' Caroline demonstrated with her hands, 'and about this big.'

I started to laugh – imagine if she said that to a teacher!

The next lot of waffles was only slightly burnt. I scraped the black bits off, wondering if I should have told Gwilliam that the book was Tal.

I dripped maple syrup on my waffle and Dad gave me my orders for the day.

They were important ones. First of all we had to get the whole house ready for Nain to come home to. That meant that I had to wash the dishes, vacuum and tidy up.

Secondly, Dad was going shopping to replace everything we'd eaten or broken.

And third, Caroline was going to buy a bunch of flowers from the flower shop.

After breakfast I had a quick bath, got dressed and started on the kitchen wearing Nain's yellow rubber gloves.

It was hard work, but a couple of hours later, the three of us stood back to admire the place. It was gleaming. I have to say it looked nearly as good as when Nain cleans it.

At lunchtime, Dad checked his watch, combed his hair and we got into the car to bring her home.

Chapter Fourteen

I thought that Nain would be waiting for us by the main entrance with her suitcase and I was disappointed when she wasn't. Dad parked around the back. Apart from birdsong, Whitehill was quiet. As we went inside, Betty, the care assistant, was on the phone at the desk, and she gave us a wave. The three of us walked up the stairs and we buzzed ourselves into the day room.

'Hey, what's happened?' Dad asked suddenly.

Sian Llewelyn was standing near Nain who was slumped in the chair in a deep sleep, her glasses half-way down her nose. Sian said reassuringly, 'It's nothing to worry about, it's just that she's very tired today, Michael.'

Dad was puzzled. 'She was fine when Dr. Hill saw her this morning,' he said, crouching down to look at his mother. 'Mam?' He patted her limp hand. 'Mam, it's Michael. We've come to take you home.'

Nain snored softly, ignoring us. She was in the deepest sleep I'd ever seen.

'In all fairness, Michael,' Sian said smugly, 'I have tried to explain to you that she's not ready to leave just yet. The idea of moving has given her a relapse.'

Poor Nain! For a moment I felt really bad for wanting her to come home.

'But Dr. Hill said it was fine for her to leave,' Dad said.

'I'm aware of what Dr. Hill said,' Sian went on patiently, 'but you can see for yourself that she's not ready.'

I didn't believe her. Nain wasn't wearing the pink cardigan - she had her best navy one on. And I looked at Nain's feet. 'She's got her black shoes on!' I said. 'She's got her shoes on because she's ready to go home.'

Sian Llewelyn turned and smiled at me. It was one of those horrible smiles that adults give you when they know they can't hit you because it's against the law.

'What I mean,' Sian said, 'is that it's exhausted her, you can see that, can't you?'

Dad frowned. 'I'm not an idiot,' he said.

I glanced at Caroline, expecting her to argue with him, but she was frowning at

Nain, probably thinking it was nothing that a smudge of lip gloss couldn't fix.

It was all a bit awkward, really.

We stood around our dozing Nain for a bit longer, hoping she would wake up.

We didn't want to go home without her, but unless we were going to carry her out, it looked as if we'd have to.

'Well,' Dad said after we watched her for a few minutes, 'I suppose we'll have to leave her here.'

'I think it's for the best. She can stay as long as she likes,' Sian said. 'When a person is old, what she needs is a secure environment and a routine.'

Just then, Nain's eyes opened a little and she blinked.

'Dad,' I said, nudging him.

'No, Sian's right, I guess.'

Nain's eyes were wide open now.

'But Dad – '

'She does seem to be happy here,' he said. 'With the secure environment and the routine.'

Sian nodded. 'Of course.'

Dad rested his hand on my head. 'Ava was going to stay with her, but obviously that's out of the question now.'

'Totally out of the question,' Sian said. 'You can't expect a kid to meet the needs of a senile old woman.'

Nain wasn't going to like that.

Sure enough, her glasses flashed. I stared at her hopefully. She hates people talking about her like that.

'So that's settled,' Sian said smoothly. 'She can stay here and live out her last days in peace.'

As Nain looked up at me I noticed little black dots forming on her glasses. They merged into a pattern that reminded me of the Blue Lagoon. The little dots were birds - I could even see their fluttering wings. There were so many tiny birds in such a small space that the glasses turned black with them and the lenses began to bulge out slowly like bubbles.

I was holding my breath, wondering what I would see next, when suddenly the lenses shattered and the bits of lens fell into Nain's lap.

I felt the breeze on my face as the birds fluttered out of her eyes like a swarm of insects and flew straight into Sian's.

As the black, lively flock engulfed her she let out a scream and started beating them away like a cloud of gnats but there were too many of them.

'MY EYEEEEEEEES!' Sian screamed.

'CALM DOWN!' Dad shouted, grabbing her flailing hands.

The old people started shouting, too; all except Nain, who was lying back in the chair, watching defiantly through her empty frames.

'THERE'S NOTHING WRONG WITH YOUR EYES!' Dad yelled, but the broken glass on Nain's lap reflected Sian's red sockets oozing thick clots of sticky blood.

Sian saw the vision too and she tried to grab Nain to put a stop to it.

So Caroline slapped Sian, hard.

The noise was like punching a deflated helium balloon - you could hear it over the frightened cries of the old people.

Sian ran sobbing to the door with her shiny hair flying behind her. She pressed the alarm button, and the bell drowned the old people out.

Caroline picked up the broken lens on Nain's knee and looked at me through a clear shard of glass. Her green eye surrounded by black Chanel eyelashes looked huge and scared. 'Did you see that? How did you *do* that?' she asked Nain.

Her fingers had blood on them and she wiped them on the carpet. 'Did you see that, Michael?'

'No,' Dad said firmly.

'Those tiny birds pecked out her eyes!'

'Nonsense,' Dad said. 'She could see the door easily enough, couldn't she?' He knelt by Nain. 'What happened, Mam? What happened?'

'My head hurts,' she said. A big tear rolled from her eye into her white hair.

I could feel my mouth wobbling.

Even Caroline looked upset. 'You need to call the doctor, Michael.'

'Right,' Dad said suddenly, and his voice seemed to explode with noise. He pointed his finger at Nain. 'Don't you worry about a thing.'

I followed him out. If I'd stayed with Nain, I knew I'd burst into tears. I followed behind him so closely along the corridor that he turned to yell at me, and we nearly fell over the stairlift.

Dad kicked it, and galloped down the stairs two at a time. I hurried after him. Betty, Tal and a care assistant came rushing across the hall towards us. 'Get Dr. Hill,' he said. 'NOW!'

He turned back up the stairs.

I trailed after him, trying not to cry.

Back in the day room, as Dad and the care assistants helped Nain to her room, I told Tal what had happened.

'Birds came out of her glasses?' he asked. 'And attacked Sian Llewelyn?'

I nodded miserably.

'Amazing!' he said.

But I shook my head. I had the same feeling that I'd had in the churchyard. I felt very small, and the world felt very big.

We waited until the doctor came. He examined Nain and said she was exhausted. Dad, who was still angry, said he could have diagnosed that himself without any help. Then he apologised, and after that, we kissed Nain goodbye and got into the car to go back home.

'In real life, Sian's eyes are all right, aren't they?' I asked, leaning forward to wedge my face between the front seats. 'They haven't really been pecked out by birds?'

'Don't be ridiculous. There's nothing wrong with her eyes,' Dad said, reversing in the car park, tyres squealing. 'Whatever Sian thought happened, it didn't. She's paying for those glasses,' he said grimly. And then he added 'The light's terrible in that day room. It's those energy saving bulbs. They're useless.'

Caroline didn't say a word. She was trying to get the blood out from under her nail.

We'd all seen the birds. And we knew that Dad had seen them too, even if he was pretending he hadn't.

Just then I saw James Dodd slinking behind a rhododendron bush in his camouflage gear. He dodged into the gardener's shed.

'There's GI Joe,' Dad said.

Neither Caroline nor I laughed.

I don't even think that Caroline heard him, because suddenly she said, 'I'm not sorry I slapped Sian Llewelyn. I don't trust her one little bit. And there's no point in lying about it, Michael; we all saw those birds.'

'If you think that, you're crazy,' Dad said firmly, and Caroline slapped him.

We spent the rest of the trip home in silence.

Back at Nain's, he pulled up at the kerb and we all got out of the car and waited as Dad unlocked the front door of Nain's house. As he did, a huge gust of wind blew through the house like an angry ghost, slamming doors behind it.

We all screamed, but Dad screamed the loudest. Then he told us to stay where we were, and he went through to the kitchen. We followed him, and I couldn't believe we'd left the place in such a mess. Then I remembered we hadn't – I remembered us all standing back to admire how neat it was, with the pink roses and everything.

'We've been ransacked,' Dad said in astonishment. 'Ransacked!'

I went into the kitchen. It was easy to see how they'd got in. One of the panes of glass in the door was broken and the key was still in the lock where Dad had left it. All Nain's pots and pans were on the kitchen floor.

'What have they taken?'

Caroline ran upstairs to check her laptop and vanity case. 'My things are still here,' she said when she came back down.

'My trophies!' shouted Dad from the lounge. I dashed in to comfort him, but he was cradling them in his arms. 'They didn't take my sporting trophies.' He looked puzzled. 'They're valuable. This one's solid silver. See? It's got a hallmark.'

'That says EPNS,' Caroline said.

'I can't believe they didn't take them,' Dad said, insulted.

'So what did they take?'

We had been living in Nain's for a week. We tried to remember what had been here before and what wasn't here any longer. Dad thought a saucepan might be missing, a small Teflon-coated one, but that was all we could come up with. It didn't seem worth ringing the police about.

'Why would they break in and not take anything?' he asked.

'Because there was nothing here that they wanted,' Caroline said. 'They would be after HD tv's, home cinemas, that sort of thing.'

'It's good news, really,' Dad said, and you could tell he was trying to look on the bright side. 'I'll get that pane mended and we'd better keep the key hidden from now on.'

We tidied up the house again. Once everything had gone back into the cupboards and drawers and it was neat, we sat around the table and Dad produced a dusty bottle of Johnny Walker Black Label.

'Whoever broke in must be a tea-totaller,' Dad said. 'Lucky for us.'

He gave us a drop each, for shock, and then he gave himself a little bit more because he'd been the first one in the house. 'We've got to work out what we're going to do now,' he said. 'I can't stay off work indefinitely.'

'Me neither,' Caroline said.

'I can still look after Nain,' I said.

For a moment, Dad didn't say anything. Then he ruffled my hair. 'You're a good girl, Ava.'

'You can't leave her at Whitehill,' I protested. 'She hates Sian Llewelyn.'

We all agreed about that.

Caroline ran her thumb around the rim of the glass. After a moment, she said, 'Why can't she go into a care home in London?'

Dad looked at her as if she was a genius.

'We could visit her whenever we wanted, and when she's better, we'll bring her back.'

'But I want her to stay here!' I said. Tal and I had to find where Brân's skull was hidden! We had to stick to the plan!

'The only birds you get in London are pigeons,' Dad said, ignoring me, 'and no-one in the history of the world has ever been scared by a pigeon. Except for you, Caroline. I'll check the Internet,' he said, and he started looking happy again. 'We could all be home by tomorrow.'

'Noooo!' That was the last thing I wanted to do.

They didn't listen.

They looked at a few care homes on Caroline's laptop and I kept my fingers crossed that they would all be full. They should have been. On the websites they were full of happy white-haired old people eating at tables with pink napkins and playing bridge. There was even one with a bar. Dad started making phone calls to find a vacancy.

'We might be lucky,' he said.

Caroline raised her eyebrows. 'It's not lucky for the person who vacated it,' she replied.

I couldn't stop thinking about Tal. 'If you find somewhere, can I stay here at Nain's by myself?' I pleaded. 'It's important. And I'll be really good.' But I knew what Dad was going to reply.

And he did.

'You're too young,' he said.

Chapter Fifteen

That evening after supper, I went round to see Tal.

His father was sitting by the table with an open can of Brasso, polishing a piece of driftwood with a t-shirt. 'Hello, kiddo,' he said, looking up from his work.

'Hello, Fred.'

Tal took me into his kitchen. You couldn't see the ceiling for dried herbs, but they smelled really nice and I started to feel hungry.

He took two Pepsis out of the fridge and gave me one. 'Sian fired me. She's wearing yellow sports glasses with elastic on the back. She's scared that the birds will get her for real.'

'I don't blame her,' I said. But it made me smile.

'I wish I could do that. If someone really annoyed me, I'd just go, hey, watch this, and squidge! I'd show them something that would freak them out!'

'It sure freaked me out,' I said truthfully.

Tal opened the cupboard doors. 'Crisps?' He gave me a bag of ready salted. 'So how did she do it? Did she make an incantation?'

'No. I just think she did it because Sian knows about the Head,' I said. 'James Dodd told me she was looking for the skull of Brân because she'd heard Idrys talking about it. Maybe she thinks Nain can help, and she doesn't want her to leave. Maybe she thinks you can help, too. Maybe that's why she asked you to work there. And the bad news is,' I said gloomily, 'my dad is looking for a care home in London, and you know what that would mean – I'd have to go back with them.'

'What about me?' Tal asked.

I felt really bad for letting him down. 'I know. But we might find out the answer before then.'

Tal shrugged and he took a slurp of Pepsi. 'Let's get on with it, then, shall we?'

So I listened to more extracts from Tal, the human book.

'Four,' he said, leaning on the fridge, 'Three Women who received Eve's beauty in third shares. Diademea, mistress of Aeneas White Shield, Elen the Magnificent and Polixena, daughter of Priam the Old, King of Troy. Five. Three Red Ravagers of this Island...Arthur, and Rhun, son of Beli, and Morgant the Wealthy. Six. Three Exalted Prisoners of the Island of Britain; Llyr two Languages who was imprisoned by Euroswydd, Mabon, son of Modron and third, Gwair, son of Geirioedd. And one prisoner was more important that these and it was Arthur. And Goreu, son of Custennin, was the same boy who released him from each of these three prisons. Seven. Three Fair Princes of the Island of Britain: Owain, son of Uriel, Rhun son of Maelgwyn and Rhufawn, the radiant son of Dewrarth Wledig. Eight...'

I watched his serious face and I couldn't believe he had spent his whole life learning about fair princes and all that. I felt sorry for him and impressed at the same time because I knew I wouldn't have done it. I wouldn't want the hard work of memorizing things.

'...Three Pillars of Battle of the Island of Britain: Dunawd, son of Pabo Pillar of

Britan and Gwallawg, son of Lleenawg and Cynfelyn the Leprous.'

'Leprosy?' I was interested in Cynfelyn the Leprous in a horrible sort of way – it's like flesh-eating bacteria – I have to read about it just in case I catch it. 'There are lepers buried under Green Park,' I said.

'Where did they come from?' Tal asked, opening his eyes.

'I forget. I think there was a leper hospital there once.'

Tal gave a half-smile. 'I've never been to London.'

'Why not?'

'It's got scvcn million people. I'd get lost in the crowds.'

I poked him with my big toe. 'They're not all out in the streets at the same time, stupid.' Maybe he wasn't that bright after all.

'I know that,' he said. 'Stupid.'

'If I did have to go back home, you could come with us.'

'Nah,' he said, but his eyes were suddenly hopeful. 'What would your dad say?'

'Well – he'd be at work.'

'And what about Caroline?'

154

'She doesn't actually live with us. Dad's too messy.'

'Okay, then, I'll come,' he said, just like that.

'Yay!!!' I couldn't believe he'd said okay!!!

Now I just had to get it sorted with Dad somehow.

'Nine,' Tal said, carrying on with the triads. 'Three horses who carried the Horse-burdens.'

'We're doing horses?'

'Black Moro, who was the horse of Elidir Mwynfawr, who carried on his back seven and a half people from Penlleth – '

'How can you have half a person?'

'And Gelbeinevin his cook, swam with his two hands to the horse's crupper – and that was the half-person. Corvan, horse of…'

What's a horse's crupper? What happened to the leprous guy?

It was like when I used to listen to The Archers with Mum. I could never concentrate on it. Nobody ever seemed to do anything exciting. And I always got the characters mixed up.

After the Three Horses came Three Roving Fleets and Three Harmful Blows, and I got cramp in my leg and rubbed it.

'Are you listening?' Tal asked me suspiciously.

'Absolutely,' I said. I was opening the crisps just as the doorbell rang.

We heard his dad answer it. I recognised my dad's voice, sounding louder than usual. Uh-oh. What had I done now?

Moments later Fred opened the kitchen door, looking irritable. 'A word, you two?'

Tal brushed the crisp crumbs from his t-shirt. 'What's up?'

'Gwilliam's here. He's brought your Dad along with him, Ava. He says you two have stolen something from Idrys. '

Tal and I looked at each other. Argh!!! I'd completely forgotten about Gwilliam.

'Oh yeah?' Tal asked his dad, 'And you believe him, do you?'

Fred beckoned us and we followed him into the lounge. Gwilliam was sitting on the sofa wearing the brown curly wig which reminded me of a red setter.

Dad was standing up, red with anger or embarrassment, or both. 'Let's get this cleared up,' he said. 'Ava – '

But Gwilliam interrupted him. 'They came into my shop interrogating me – interrogating me about Idrys's book,' he repeated, looking at Fred and Dad, 'and lying – lying, isn't that so, Ava - about a school project?'

My face burned.

'You've been interrogating him and lying about school?' Dad asked me, appalled.

'And,' Gwilliam went on before I could answer, 'I made the mistake – I admit it was a mistake – of telling them how valuable this book is likely to be; and to put it into perspective, Michael, this book is so valuable as to be invaluable, you understand? It has to be returned.'

'Where's the book, Tal?' Fred asked sternly, appalled that it was invaluable.

We all looked at Tal.

I waited for him to say he was the Book, because how stupid was Gwilliam going to look when he told them that?

But he didn't. 'Even if I had the book, I couldn't tell you,' he said to Gwilliam, flicking away his fringe. 'You were his friend. If he kept if from you it's because he didn't want you to know about it.'

I cringed, because, let's face it, he was just making things worse.

Dad cleared his throat and pushed Fred out of the way. 'Where's the book, Ava?'

Oh, great. It was like Dad wars – a competition to see which father could make his child tell first. But I couldn't say anything, could I? Not if Tal wasn't. I shrugged.

'I'm sorry to say that this, then, is a police matter,' Gwilliam said, getting to his feet.

'No,' Dad said. 'Wait, Gwilliam. Ava? I'm going to count to ten and then...'

When I didn't say anything, he said, 'What? Do you want a criminal record at your age?'

I didn't. 'You can call the police but we haven't got anything that belongs to Idrys, honestly, Dad.'

'You told me this morning that you'd found it,' Gwilliam said, scratching under wig.

'That was because I didn't want Dad to know I lied about the school project.'

'Right,' Dad said, going red again, 'I'll deal with that later. Now listen Gwilliam, you heard them. They haven't got the book. BUT,' he added, pointing at me, 'if you do find it, you're to give to straight to me.'

Gwilliam didn't look very happy with that idea.

'If I can explain about the Head of Brân, Michael,' he said breathlessly, 'you will see why the Book is valuable. It contains the whereabouts of the sacred Head of Blessed Brân from the sixth century AD which has great powers. It protects the country.'

Dad groaned and pressed his eyes. 'Gwilliam, sorry and all that, but I've had it up to here with that kind of thing,' he said.

Fred looked from Dad to Gwilliam. 'Is there anything else, Gwilliam?' he asked, politely. 'I've got work to do.'

'So have I,' Dad said.

'Profuse apologies,' Gwilliam said, bowing to Dad and Fred in turn. 'So, Michael, I will expect to hear from you if and when. That book is worth a fortune, you know.'

He ignored us altogether. Tal and I looked at each other, relieved that the whole horrible business was settled.

'See you, Fred,' Dad said in solidarity, following Gwilliam to the door. 'Come on, Ava.'

'But –'

'NOW.'

Reluctantly I said goodbye to Tal and followed Dad out, going over it all in my mind – Gwilliam saying we'd stolen something and Dad's face when he heard about my lies and interrogations – and I knew I was going to be in big trouble when I got home.

Chapter Sixteen

I was right, I did get into big trouble. Dad lectured me for half an hour and used the word 'disappointed' a lot. I was relieved when he finally sent me to bed.

I sat in the attic, longing to ring Rosie to moan about him. Even though I didn't have any credit, I wanted my mobile. But I couldn't find it. I looked under the bed. I couldn't understand it - I knew it had been under my pillow. I remembered putting it there. And now it had gone. What if it had been stolen by the person who broke in?

Who had broken in?

Gwilliam, I thought in a sudden flash of inspiration. He'd broken in to look for the non-existent book.

But how did he know we'd be out?

Oh yes… I'd told him.

And then he'd stolen my phone.

Which is pink.

Hmmm… the thing is, even though I hated him for getting me into trouble, and even though I've got a good imagination, I just couldn't imagine Gwilliam doing it. I couldn't imagine him breaking a window or ransacking the place – what if he'd been caught? He'd have to go to court and people would stop buying his books.

It would have to be someone who thought they could sell a pink phone, I thought sadly, wondering if I would ever get it back. It would have to be a person who wasn't scared of anyone and who was a fast runner. Someone like James Dodd when I saw him sneaking into the gardener's shed at Whitehill.

Yikes!!!

I waited until Dad and Caroline went to bed, and then I crept down the stairs, holding my breath and praying they wouldn't creak too loudly and I ran up the road to Tal's.

Yes, I know it was a stupid thing to do, but I wanted my phone back.

I stood outside his house in the dark and threw earth at his window. I'm hopeless at throwing, so quite a bit of it went on his porch roof, but eventually his curtains moved and I saw his face appear.

Five minutes later he was outside too.

'Has your dad chucked you out?' he whispered.

'I wish.' I explained about the break-in and about my phone and about James going furtively into the gardener's shed.

'I thought it was something important,' he said.

'It is! It's not the first one I've lost.'

'Why would James Dodd break into your Nain's and steal your phone?'

'Well first I thought it might have been Gwilliam, looking for the Book.' We tiptoed back past Nain's house. 'But then,' I carried on, 'I couldn't really imagine him doing anything reckless like that. I mean – he got our dads involved. He'd get the police involved too, if he thought it would help.'

'Maybe James Dodd was looking for the Book.'

'He doesn't know anything about it.'

'He found the list, didn't he?'

'Oh, yes.' I blushed. That list! I wished I'd never written it – it had caused me nothing but trouble. 'Anyway,' I said, avoiding the subject, 'I think he hid my phone in the shed and I'm going to find it.'

'Did you bring a torch?'

'No.'

I saw car lights sweep the road, and we pressed against the wall until it passed.

'Lucky I've got my lighter with me,' Tal commented.

We hurried up to the electronic gate which was, of course, locked. At the bottom of the drive, Whitehill glowed with soft lights, but the entrance hall was dark. I climbed over first, and jumped down onto the drive. 'Hurry up.'

We walked through the oak trees. The black night was full of rustlings and scuttlings, and gossamer clung to my face. I tried not to think of spiders, or of getting caught. As we crossed the dewy grass towards the car park, I could see the dark bundle of rhododendron bushes and the angled roof of the tool shed.

Hunched up, we crept towards it stealthily, like shadows.

And then the security lights switched on, dazzling us. We froze to the spot.

Tal swore, in Welsh, and, totally blinded, we dived into the bushes.

Hiding in the leaves I was too deafened by my heartbeat to hear anything, and I tried to blink the purple and yellow blobs out of my eyes.

Suddenly the kitchen light went on.

I peered through the branches and saw Sian Llewelyn come to the window.

She cupped her hands around her sports glasses and looked out. I was trembling so much that all the leaves in the bush around me were shaking.

She stayed there for what seemed like ages, and then the security light switched off.

Seconds later, the kitchen light switched off, too, and we were in the bush in pitch blackness again.

'Tal?'

'I think I've had a heart attack,' he said.

I started to giggle.

'Shhh. We'll have to go round the back of the shed so that we don't trigger the sensors, okay?'

'Okay.' I crawled out and brushed myself down. I was itching all over. I bet I was covered in insects. 'Tal?'

'I'm here,' he said.

It was pitch black behind the shed. Suddenly I walked into something hard and cold. 'Ow!'

Tal bumped into me. 'What's happened?'

'Hang on, I just banged my knee,' I whispered. I felt the top of the hard cold object and touched something soft and sticky.

There was a click, and Tal's face lit up in the glow of his lighter. He held it out in front of him. 'It's the sun dial,' he said. 'What's that lying on top of it?'

As Tal brought his lighter closer I could see it was a dead pigeon. I jerked my hand away. The worse thing was, it wasn't just dead; its insides had been pulled out and were glistening on the ruffled feathers like worms in a pool of blood.

Pierced on the finger of the sundial was a note with SUCCESSFUL ENTERPRISE written on it in huge black letters.

'RUN!' Tal said, and he took off across the grass, leaving me behind.

I forgot all about my phone. I'm not a good runner, but I was so scared that I overtook him by the oak trees, and we scrambled over the gate together and ran down the road, only stopping when we reached Nain's. We shivered breathlessly outside her neighbours' house.

'What the hell was that?' I asked at last.

'You don't want to know.'

For a moment I agreed with him. And then I said bravely, 'Yes, I do.'

'Sian Llewelyn's reading the future through dying animals,' Tal said. 'Druids used to do that a long time ago.'

'Oh.' I stared at his worried face. 'And it's all good, isn't it? Successful enterprise.'

Tal looked grim under the glow of the street light. 'Not for us, it isn't. Whatever she's got planned, it's going to work out just fine,' he said.

chapter seventeen

I didn't sleep very well after that.

Next day Dad still wasn't talking to me because of the Gwilliam trouble. So from Caroline I found out that:

1. Dad had sorted Nain a care home in London, and

2. We were all going home as soon as we'd packed.

'I don't want to go home,' I said to Caroline. 'I can't go home.'

Caroline looked at me. And I looked at her. Her blonde hair was messy, as it always was in the morning, and she hadn't put her make-up on yet. She looked friendlier without it.

'Why can't you go home?'

'Because,' I said desperately.

I didn't know what else to tell her, and while I was trying to work out a reason for staying that she would believe, which didn't involve Heads, druids and dead birds, she said softly, 'You sneaked out last night, didn't you?'

168

My heart skipped a beat, but at least she hadn't told my dad. Yet.

I nodded, dreading what was going to come next.

'Did you meet up with Tal?'

I nodded again.

'Thought so,' she said.

'The thing is, I thought I was coming for the whole summer,' I explained, 'and we've planned to do things and Dad won't let me stay.'

Caroline nodded and chewed her gum thoughtfully. 'If you can't stay here in Wales,' she said after a moment, 'why doesn't Tal come back to London with us?'

'I know, but Dad won't agree to that.'

Caroline was thoughtful for a moment. Then she said, 'Ask him. You've got nothing to lose.'

So I did.

And of course, he said no.

He was packing, and he couldn't fit everything in the car boot. Our bags seemed to be bigger, going back.

'Please?'

'No.'

'Pleease!'

'No.'

I followed him downstairs.

Caroline had the red chopsticks in her hair and she was buffing her nails by the table, to make them shiny.

'Dad – '

'Ava, don't ask me again!' Dad warned me, jamming his shaver into his sponge bag.

'But – '

'No, and THAT'S FINAL!' he yelled.

I sat on the chair with my chin in my hands, feeling as if it was the end of the world. It *was* going to be the end of the world, or at least the country, and it was all my dad's fault.

All he was worried about was getting annoyed with his shaver which had switched itself on inside the bag.

Caroline began buffing the other hand. Without looking at him, she said, 'Ava'll be at home all day by herself, Michael; have you thought of that?'

Dad grunted.

'What are you going to do about it?' she asked him.

'I'll think of something,' he said.

'You could hire an au pair for her.'

'Hey!' I jumped out of my seat indignantly. Why was she putting ideas like that into his head?

'Or a minder.'

'What?'

'Or a bodyguard? Get her a bodyguard,' Caroline said.

'She's not that bad,' Dad said, zipping his sponge bag up, finally.

Actually I liked the idea of a bodyguard. All pop stars had bodyguards. 'Get one with sunglasses,' I said. 'And a gun.'

'Don't be ridiculous,' Dad said, getting cross. 'You don't need one. You're perfectly capable of looking after yourself.'

'But I'll be bored.'

'Bored? Bored?' He was all worked up again. 'I was never bored when I was your age. I was on the go from morning 'til night. There are plenty of things you can do. You've got friends, haven't you?'

'I guess.' I looked up at him hopefully. 'Can Tal come back with us?'

'Yes,' Dad said after a second's hesitation. 'But I'll have to speak to his parents.'

I looked at Caroline. She was still buffing her nails. She was a genius!!!

Tal's parents gave Dad two hundred pounds, 'for food and expenses'.

Two hundred pounds!

'Send him back when you get tired of him,' Fred said.

I could see Dad looking at Fred's suit.

I could see Fred looking at Dad's navy golf shirt.

Tal was standing next to his navy backpack. He'd cut his hair and now it was short all over and less blonde. He looked older. And one side of his face was paler where his fringe had been and it looked a bit strange. Like the Phantom of the Opera. It would probably catch up, I thought, when the sun got to it.

We went to Whitehill to pick up Nain.

Betty came to say goodbye and James Dodd pushed her to the car in a wheelchair.

'London,' he sneered, looking into the car through his long, dark eyelashes.

Sian Llewelyn was standing in the doorway with her yellow sports glasses fixed firmly on her face. Nain's strange powers had scared her and she wasn't taking any chances.

Nain was very cheerful about leaving. She squashed in the back seat between me and Tal. She said she felt safer with 'the young ones' because she didn't trust Dad's driving.

'I heard that,' Dad said.

'You were meant to,' she replied. Then we took her home.

She looked around her house and praised us for taking good care of it, and she packed some clothes. Then we all squashed in the car again and Tal and I had to hold our bags on our laps because there wasn't enough room in the boot.

We were almost on the bypass when Dad remembered he'd left the immersion heater on, and we went back once more.

Nain said she'd go to the bathroom one last time, and it made me want to go, so in the end we all went one last time, except Dad, who said he could last a measly two hours.

'Two hours? What speed will you be driving at?' Nain asked sharply.

And then we motored towards the bypass again.

Chapter Eighteen

When we reached North London it was evening and the sun was setting. Dad parked up at the top of Highgate Hill and got out to stretch his legs. 'Look at that, Tal,' he said. In the distance we could see the city skyline, gold in the sun from east to west. We all got out of the car, except Nain, and stood on the pavement to look.

'See Telecom Tower and the London Eye, Tal?' Dad said. 'And over there, to the left, St. Paul's? And the Gherkin,' he said, pointing. 'And the Tower of London. See?'

I couldn't see any sign of flames or smoke and I felt a lot happier.

Tal stood in silence with his hands in his pockets, probably worrying about losing himself in a crowd of seven million people.

'What a great sight!' Dad said happily, as if he'd been away for months. He sounded relieved to be nearly home.

I felt like that, too. We were back to our normal lives.

We got back into the car. Dad dropped Tal and me off home, and he gave me the house keys and twenty pounds, and said to order a takeaway, the usual for him, and he would microwave it when he got back. Then he and Caroline took Nain to the Woodlands Care Home.

It felt really strange being back. There was a pile of letters on the mat when I opened the door, but nothing for me. I don't know why I bother looking.

I showed Tal round, and our feet echoed on the wood floors. Everything seemed different, as if I hadn't remembered it properly. 'This is the lounge,' I said. The red rug was crooked and I straightened it and checked the fish. They swam out of the skull and gobbled the fish flakes greedily. I took Tal upstairs, feeling like an estate agent. 'This is your room.' Tal put his backpack inside the door. 'And this is my room.' It was untidy; I'd forgotten that. I closed the door quickly. 'That one's Dad's. And that's the bathroom.'

We went back downstairs and I took one of Fong's Chinese menus from the kitchen cupboard for Tal to choose his supper. I knew what I was having. 'I always have crispy chilli beef,' I told him, 'but you have to order it slowly, or else they give you crispy seaweed.' Mr Fong is from Hong Kong.

Tal chose the Special House Curry, and we ordered egg fried rice and prawn crackers and lemon chicken for Dad.

I laid the table and we went into the lounge and waited for the food to come.

Twenty minutes later, Mr Fong's son arrived, carrying a white plastic bag. I paid with Dad's money, and Tal and I took it into the kitchen.

I was hungry, and Fong's crispy chilli beef is the best in the world. It's also got carrots and onions in it, so it's healthy, too. I'd eat it for every meal if Dad would let me.

Tal liked his Special House curry. 'It's got prawns, pork, beef and chicken,' he said. 'It's four meals in one.'

After we'd eaten we took our drinks into the lounge and sat on the red sofa.

Tal said that his brain was working better after the food, and took a deep breath. 'Ready?'

'Yeah, I'm ready,' I said, putting a cushion behind me.

'Arthur's Three Great Mistresses,' he said. 'Indeg, daughter of Garwy the Tall; Garwen Fair Leg, daughter of Henin the Old; and Gwyl Modest, daughter of Gendawd Big Chin.'

Fancy being called Gendawd Big Chin! I wouldn't be a druid if you paid me.

I started dreaming up names for my friends. Rosie would be Rosie Wide Eyes and Zoe would be Zoe the Short. I would be Ava the … Bather, why not.

'…Three frivolous Bards of the Island of Britain: Arthur, and Cadwallawn and Rahawd, son of Morgant. Nine. Three Fortunate Concealments of the Island of Britain: The Head of Brân the Blessed, son of Llyr, which was concealed in the White Hill in London, with its face towards France.' Tal nearly kicked the can out of my hand. 'Ava!' His eyes were popping out of his head.

'What? What?'

'…The Head of Brân the Blessed, son of Llyr, which was concealed in the White Hill in London, with its face towards France. And as long as it was in the position it was put there, no disaster would ever come to this Island! White Hill! The

White Hill in London,' Tal said excitedly. 'Where's that?'

'Great!' I was excited, too. 'I know Whitehall.'

'It's not Whitehall, it's White Hill.'

'How about Whiteleys?'

'White HILL,' Tal said as though I was deaf.

'Hill... I know Primrose Hill. And Parliament Hill.'

'AVA!' he yelled.

I got offended. 'What am I – a human atlas? I Don't Know Where It Is!!! But,' I added more calmly, 'we could look it up in the A to Z.'

'Yes?' he said doubtfully.

'It's not like yours,' I reassured him. The A to Z for Ruabon is really funny. It's got a few streets in it, and lots of bare bits. 'London's pretty well all streets. It's bound to be in it.' I gave him the London A-Z from the bookcase.

Tal flicked through it, mumbling to himself.

'WhiteAcre...Whiteadder...Whitebarn ...White Bear... White Butts.' He grinned. 'White Butts! ...Whitechapel... White City... White Friars...White

Head…White Heron… Whitehorn. That's it?' Tal asked, getting all worked up. 'From Heron to Horn? No White Hill? There are white bears and friars and harts and feet and no hill? What's that all about?'

'See!' I said. 'There isn't one.'

'White Horse, White Oak,' Tal said, 'White Lion. How weird is that?' He looked at me over the book. 'Don't you think it's weird there's a white everything but not a White Hill?'

I shrugged.

'*I* think it's weird,' he said.

I took the A-Z from him and looked through it myself. He was right, there were a lot of places with White in them. I thought of Idrys writing Gwyn Fryn all over his window. We'd thought it meant Whitehill, the nursing home, but it was White Hill, two words. It had been a clue!

Tal was looking out of the window and I stood next to him and leant on the window sill. Beyond us, the huge city glittered brightly in the dark like LED lights on a board.

'Somewhere out there is a White Hill,' Tal said softly, 'with the Head of Brân hidden in it. Now all we have to do is find it.'

Sometime during the night, I dreamt of a white hill near a big river in the countryside. My granddad was climbing up it, which was strange, because he's dead.

I woke up and thought about my granddad. The dream was so real I could still smell his hair gel. His name was Gwynne, and I knew why I'd dreamt about him – Gwyn Fryn. White Hill.

But he used to say that his name meant pure or blessed.

For a moment I felt excited even though I was half asleep. Maybe it wasn't White Hill but Blessed Hill! I could go downstairs and look it up in the A-Z! Any...second...now...

And I fell asleep again.

When Dad came downstairs dressed for work the next morning he was surprised to see Tal and me in the kitchen.

'There's no food,' I said accusingly, shutting the fridge door.

'You'd better have some money to get some,' he said, frowning and taking out his wallet. 'Here's fifty. And Tal...' he counted out another fifty. 'This is to be going on with. Do something – '

'Educational?' Tal suggested, stuffing it into his brown wallet.

'Yeah, educational with it,' Dad said, looking relieved.

Fifty pounds! I could see Dad looking at the clock and then at us. He had to get to work.

'Don't go getting into mischief,' he said.

'We won't,' Tal said, as though he meant it.

'And if you need anything –'

'I'll call you,' I promised. ''Bye, Dad.'

'Fifty pounds each!' I said to Tal as soon as he'd left.

'But we have to buy food with it.'

'Not with all of it. And we could buy cheap food. Like Pot Noodles.'

'And beans. I like beans.'

Suddenly, I remembered my dream about my grandfather and I hurried to get the A-Z while I told Tal about my theory.

He was excited, too.

I traced down the Bs with my finger, and then down the Ps. But disappointingly, there was no Blessed Hill or Pure Hill in London. Not one. So that was that. I put the A-Z on the table.

'Have a look for Holy Hill,' Tal suggested.

I found a Holly Hill, in Hampstead. I didn't think that was it. 'My hill was by a river,' I said, 'I know it was just a dream but it felt real. Only it wasn't in the city. It was the countryside.'

'I suppose London must have been all countryside once, centuries ago,' Tal said.

'That's true. There used to be highwaymen up on Hampstead Lane when it was in the middle of nowhere and when they caught them, they hung their bodies in the trees until they turned to skeletons and fell apart, to put other highwaymen off. It says so on the wall of the Spaniards Inn.' I got quite excited, telling him, but it didn't get us anywhere. Plus, it was bit hard to concentrate. Part of my mind kept thinking of £50 and the fact I hadn't had breakfast.

'So, centuries ago,' Tal said, 'London was totally different.'

'Totally.'

Tal and I looked at each other.

'So what we need is – '

'- a centuries-old map!'

'Like a treasure map!'

'Yeah,' I said, wondering where on earth we could find a shop that sold ancient maps. Arghhhhh!!! It didn't seem fair. Every time we came up with the answer to one problem, it just led us to a new one.

Just then, the phone rang, and it was Rosie!

I went upstairs to my room to talk, because I wanted to tell her about Tal, and I couldn't while he was watching me.

I'd better describe her. She's tall, with long brown hair and wide-spaced eyes that Caroline says are attractive, but which Rosie thinks makes her look like a frog. But she says it's a good thing for a model to look a bit unusual. She's got loads of confidence.

I lay on my bed and told her about Nain's feet, and about how she couldn't look after me, and about Tal coming back with me, and that he was a druid.

'Does he wear a long brown bathrobe thing?'

I propped myself up on my pillow. 'No! Why would he? That's monks.'

'Oh.' She sounded a bit disappointed. 'What does he wear?'

'Black jeans and a black t-shirt.'

'Does he wear a black cloak the rest of the time?'

'No.'

Somewhere in the background I could hear Rosie's mother saying something to her.

'WHAT?' Rosie yelled back. 'NO, I'M NOT GOING TO GET SOME FRESH AIR.

'WHAT?

'HAVE YOU SEEN THE WEATHER? IT'S SUNNY! WHAT DO YOU WANT ME TO DO, GET SKIN CANCER?'

She nearly deafened me!

'He sounds geeky,' she said when she came back on the phone.

'Well, he's not.' I was a bit annoyed. 'He knows all the history of the Druids off by heart,' I said. I didn't think there was anything wrong in telling her that. Wales seemed a really long way away at the time. And so did Sian Llewelyn.

Rosie wasn't impressed. 'Like I said, geeky,' she said after a moment's silence. 'What shall we do today?'

'Tal and I are looking for an ancient map in the interests of national security. We've got to find a -' I was going to say a Head, but that sounded too weird. 'A skull,' I said instead.

'Okay, so after you've found it, come round. Switch your phone on, will you?'

'My phone's been stolen,' I said, and I was just going to tell the whole story when she shouted,

'MUUUUM!!!! AVA IS COMING ROUND TO OURS THIS AFTERNOON!!! OKAY??? She says yes. I've got to go now, I'm making brownies. I'll keep you one.'

I went back downstairs and Tal was still sitting at the table.

'These ancient maps,' he said. 'How much do they cost?'

'I don't know, I've never bought one. Generally there's no point in having an ancient map, is there? It's not as if you'd be lost without it. You'd be lost with it.

Anyway, we don't want to buy one. We just want to look at it.'

'We could go to the British Library, couldn't we?'

I wished I'd thought of that. 'Does it have maps?'

'It has books, doesn't it? So it'll have atlases, right? Let's borrow the oldest one that they've got of London, and find out where the White Hill used to be.'

Once we got to the British Library information desk, we found out a lot of facts that we hadn't known before.

One of them was, it had a Map Library containing four million maps.

Four million maps!

How did we know where to start?

The answer to that is, we didn't get the chance to.

The woman behind the desk stuck a pen behind her ear and said that we weren't allowed to look at old maps of London.

I pointed out that it was the British Library, and we were British.

She said that we couldn't look at them despite the fact that we were British. The only way we could see them was to apply in advance and go with a responsible adult who had a pass to the reading rooms.

'What are we, time travellers?' I said. 'How could we ask in advance? That would have to be, like, a week ago. We only thought of it today. Okay,' I said hopefully, 'can we borrow your oldest atlas of London?'

'Sorry,' she said. 'Same rules. You have to have a pass for the reading room. And you'd have to have a responsible adult with you, as you're under eighteen. Like a teacher,' she added.

'It's the summer holidays,' I said, resting my hands on the counter. 'I don't have anything to do with teachers in the summer.'

She looked sympathetic. 'Have you looked at our digital resources? A lot of our collections are scanned.'

'Are any of them maps of London?'

'Yes,' she said, and pointed us towards the PCs on the next level.

Tal and I went up the escalators and squashed onto a plastic chair in front of a free monitor and looked up London: A Life in Maps.

You'd be amazed at how many ancient maps of London there are. A hundred and forty-six thousand, six hundred and seventy-eight, to be exact. I was relieved we hadn't gone to the reading room with a responsible adult, after all. Especially not my dad. He'd have looked through a couple and then said we should have a coffee. Then after the coffee he would have looked at a couple more and said he'd come back when he's retired. He's like that. He gets bored quickly.

The maps were nothing like our maps. They were more like drawings. Some had pictures of buildings on them, some were orientated east, some were written in Latin and some were coloured in by hand. We looked at them for ages while Tal zoomed in and out, randomly reading out street names.

After a while I started to get impatient. 'Maybe we should look for somewhere by a river,' I said, 'like in my dream.'

The good thing about Tal being a druid was that he believed in dreams. 'Yeah,' he agreed.

'So why don't we just look along the Thames, otherwise we'll be here all day and I promised I'd see Rosie.'

Tal went back to John Leake's map from 1666. That's the benefit of having a good memory. He zoomed in on all the sections of the map along the river. It was amazing how many hills there were. 'St Andrews Hill,' Tal said, moving east. 'Adle Hill. St – what – Bennett's Hill? St Peter's Hill. Lambert Hill. Bread Street

Hill. Garlick Hill. College Hill. Dowgate Hill. That's it on the hills – now we're on alleys.'

'There's a hill,' I said, pointing to the eastern edge of the picture. 'Tower Hill. That's because that walled building is the Tower of London.'

Tal zoomed in on the Tower. We could see the trees John Leake had drawn around it.

He zoomed out again so that we could see the entire picture. 'That part of it there is called the White Tower, look. The White Tower. Maybe it was called that because it was built on the White Hill.'

'But it's on Tower Hill,' I argued.

'Yes, dummy, but what was it called before the Tower was built? Let's look at that plan of the Roman walls.'

He clicked up the map. We hadn't looked at it closely because it was faded and you had to focus hard to read it. 'These are the walls,' he said, 'and here's the river. Look, there's the bend in it, so here's…'

'White Hill,' I said, and my skin prickled all over. Tal and I looked at each other.

He said eagerly, 'What if, because of the legend, the White Tower was built to protect the Head? I mean, it's obvious that an important holy relic would be somewhere really secure.'

We stared at each other.

'So you think the Head is in the Tower of London?'

'Yes. That's exactly what I think,' Tal said. 'Now we just need to find it. What's the time?'

I checked my watch. 'Three fifteen.'

'I'm going to buy a compass,' Tal said, 'because we know the Head faces towards France, which is roughly south-east of London. And we'll need a strong bag to hide the Head in so it doesn't get damaged.'

'Okay,' I agreed, trying not to imagine carrying around a Head in a bag. 'Let's go to Rosie's first.'

'You go to Rosie's, and I'll buy the compass,' he said. 'I'll meet you back at your house.'

We agreed to meet at home at four-thirty.

I went to the British Library basement to ring Rosie to tell her I was coming.

She picked the phone up straight away. 'Ava!!! I've been trying to get hold of you for ages!!!'

I held the handset away from my ear. 'Yeah, thing is – '

'Where are you???'

'I'm at the British Library. We know where the Head is,' I said. 'It's at the Tower of London.'

'When are you coming to my house??? I've got a surprise for you!!!'

'I'll be twenty minutes,' I said, wondering what on earth the surprise could be.

When I got to Rosie's she was bouncing on the spot with excitement. She had loads of make-up on, and a short, tight, grey dress with black tights. She looked really nice.

She said, 'Look what I've got!' and pushed something pink in my face. 'Your phone!'

'What?' As I took it from her, I thought it was a joke because how could it be my phone? But it was.

'SURPRISE!!!!' Rosie squealed so loudly and I squealed so loudly back that for a moment I didn't look at the person coming into her kitchen wearing camouflage gear, taking off his khaki baseball cap and running his hand through his black hair.

James Dodd!!!

'Surprised?' he asked.

Surprised? I nearly fell over in shock.

What was he doing in my best friend's house?

'What are you doing here?' I asked him.

James grinned, showing his perfect white teeth.

With those and the long dark eyelashes, he should have been in a boy band. He was gorgeous.

But I didn't trust him one bit.

'No! No! Let me tell her! Let me!' Rosie said. 'Guess what? He got my number from your mobile and we got talking and he came all the way here to give it back to you!'

James pushed his hands into the pockets of his combat trousers. 'Aren't you going to thank me?'

I felt my body prickling all over. 'No, I'm not! You stole it,' I said indignantly.

'I didn't steal it; I borrowed it.'

'What?' Rosie's voice went higher. 'You stole her phone? You didn't tell me that! You said you found it!'

'I did find it,' he said.

'Yeah, under my pillow.'

'What?' Rosie said, looking confused

'And you trashed my Nain's house.'

'I didn't trash it,' he said. 'It's not as if I broke anything!'

'I don't understand.' Rosie looked puzzled. 'You said you were friends!'

'We are friends,' James said.

I looked at him as if he was crazy. 'No, we're not!' And then I wished I hadn't said it, because he had a hurt look on his face which made me feel really bad.

'Look,' he said, 'where's Tal? I've got to talk to him. It's really important. It's about Sian.'

Rosie started eating one of the brownies she'd made. She can eat anything and never put on weight.

'He's back at my house,' I said reluctantly.

'Come on,' he said. 'Take me there.'

Rosie put on some more lip gloss and the three of us walked to the bus stop and caught the bus home.

Tal was sitting on the step, waiting for me to get back.

When he saw us, he stood up and shielded his eyes from the sun.

He and James stared at each other on the doorstep.

'What are *you* doing here?'

'He's going to explain all that in a minute,' I said calmly, unlocking the door. We went into the kitchen and sat around the table as if we were in a business meeting. We all looked at James.

He twisted his cap back to front. 'See, Sian wants the Head and what I was thinking was, we could do a deal. When you find it you could share it with her,' he said.

'We're not sharing the Head,' Tal said. 'Anyway, what does she want it for?'

James raised his dark eyebrows. 'She's sick of old people. She says they're more trouble than she thought. She wants Whitehill all to herself again.'

'What's the deal you want to make?'

'Us lot together, we're strong. We could do stuff. Change history. Get famous.'

'How?'

'I'll tell you when you get us the Head.'

'James, we're not sharing the Head.'

James gave us a dazzling smile. 'Think about it. Anyway,' he said, 'what do you want it for?'

'We don't want it for ourselves,' Tal said. 'We're going to protect it.'

'You're a real do-gooder. Makes no difference in the long run; we're going to get it anyway.'

'Successful enterprise.' I shivered, thinking of the dead pigeon.

James Dodd looked at me with his deep blue eyes. 'Yeah,' he agreed, 'successful enterprise. You can make it easy or make it hard, but either way we're going to win. Sorry, Ava.'

'Your dad will kill you if you get into trouble with the police again,' Tal warned. 'That Head's valuable.'

I thought of the archdruid's megaphone voice. 'You really wouldn't want him yelling at you.'

'I'm used to it,' James said. 'He's always yelling because I'm no good. But,' he grinned slowly, 'he'll soon find out what I am good at.'

I didn't like the sound of that. 'You could help us save the country! There'll be rewards! Probably,' I added, because I didn't know that for sure.

'Save the country?' James asked scornfully. 'For what?' He leant back in his chair. 'Look, if you give us the Head, you'll be safe, I guarantee it. If not….' He shrugged.

'Don't listen to him, Ava,' Tal said. 'He doesn't even know where the Head is.'

'Yes I do. It's in The Tower of London.'

We stared at him in shock. 'How do you know that?'

'You didn't say it was a secret,' Rosie said in a small voice.

James put his arm around her shoulders. 'Don't worry, Rosie. Be on my side. You could be famous this time next week.'

For a moment Rosie looked tempted and I didn't blame her. She looked from him to us, and after a moment, she said, 'Sorry James, but no thanks.'

'Okay.' He pushed back his chair and got to his feet. 'I gave you a chance,' he said angrily, raking his fingers through his dark hair. 'When it all blows up, I want you all to remember that. I gave you a chance to be friends with me.'

And then he left, slamming the door behind him.

Chapter Twenty

Early next morning, Tal and I got off the tube at Tower Hill to visit the Tower of London. The sky was grey and heavy with rain clouds.

The thing about living in London is that you never do the touristy things, mainly because if you live here, you're not a tourist. So I'd forgotten what the Tower of London looked like. I'd forgotten that it was huge, and that it had high, thick stone walls surrounding it, and I'd forgotten about the grassy moat around it and how close it was to the Thames.

'It's a castle,' Tal said. 'Why is it called a tower?'

'I don't know.'

'Where's the tower?'

'What am I, a tourist guide?' I said as we joined the queue to buy the tickets.

After we bought the tickets, we had to queue again to have our bags searched. Tal's backpack was empty because we were going to carry the shopping in it, and the Head too, if we found it. I wondered if we would get searched on the way out

Finally we were inside the huge walls of the Tower, shuffling behind a crowd of people without actually knowing where we were going.

'Why are there so many soldiers about?' Tal asked.

'They're protecting the Crown Jewels.'

'Why doesn't Securicor do it?' He stopped dead in his tracks and a German family walked into us, nearly knocking us over and causing a pile-up.

'Ach! Zo sorry,' the dad said, hitting himself on the forehead even though it was Tal's fault.

Tal didn't even seem to notice. He grabbed me by the arm. 'Listen! What can you hear?'

'Stop asking me questions,' I said, getting annoyed. But this time, he knew the answer.

'Ravens!' he said. He started pushing his way through the crowd and I hurried to keep up with him. He turned left towards a raised grassy area, and loud and clear I heard a familiar: PRRUK! PRRUK!

We were behind a short metal barrier. A sign said: BEWARE! THESE BIRDS BITE!

Behind it on the grassy bank, three big, glossy ravens were coming towards us with their bills open wide.

I wasn't sure that the barrier was enough to keep them in. It was only as high as my knees. 'They need a bigger barrier,' I said, and just at that moment Tal stepped over it and walked towards the birds. 'Tal! Come back!'

Too late. The biggest bird spread its wings like a black cloak, and ruffled its neck feathers. He took a run at Tal and his beak looked wickedly sharp but Tal stood his ground and it came to a stop in front of him. Tal stretched his arms out, and as the raven charged again, Tal moved position so that his back was to the sun, and his dark shadow spread over the ground.

The raven folded its wings swiftly and stared at Tal as if it was waiting for something.

Suddenly I heard a yell.

'Hey! You!'

A Yeoman Warder was hurrying through the crowd towards us. His tunic was black and red and he had black hair and deep angry lines on his face.

'Get off there, you fool - those birds are dangerous. Get off that grass NOW!'

I knew we would get into trouble.

Tal turned. His body was still bent and his arms were still outstretched. He looked crazy. As he walked towards us the ravens followed him, spreading their wings like cloaks behind them.

'Okay, lad, okay,' the Yeoman said. 'Easy does it, take your time. We don't want them coming into the crowd.'

Tal gave the ravens a final glance and then he ran to the barrier and jumped over it, leaving the birds croaking and strutting behind him.

The angry Yeoman introduced himself as the Ravenmaster and told him to go and stand by the wall for a 'little chat'.

That meant a long telling-off, in other words, so while I was waiting for Tal to be told off I sat on a wooden bench by the grey stone wall. Looking down, I noticed it was next to a semi-circular well, like a half-moon, covered with a metal grille.

The water at the bottom of it was green. I wouldn't have drunk from it, not even if it was the olden days - I bet it came straight from the Thames.

There was a narrow shelf about three feet down the well and it was covered in coins. I leant over the arm of the bench to get a better look. Wow! There was a heap of money down there! Mostly tens, but some fifty pences, too. Altogether there was at least five pounds. What a waste!

I stuck my fingers in the grille and it lifted straight out. I propped it against the wall. By now, my heart was beating really quickly and I wasn't sure what to do next. It wasn't actually stealing, was it? People had thrown that money away!

But I couldn't very well lie on the floor and get the coins out, not with so many people around. I had enough to worry about as it was. I pushed the bench back over it for two reasons, firstly to hide the money, and secondly, to save someone falling into the well and drowning.

Then I wandered over to Tal, who was still being told off.

'Finally,' the Ravenmaster was saying, 'for our sake, if not for yours, stay away from the ravens. You know why we keep the ravens at the Tower?'

Tal shrugged.

'Because if the ravens leave the Tower, the White Tower will collapse and a great disaster will befall the nation.'

Tal and I gasped in surprise!

That was exactly the story as the legend of Brân's Head!

Lecture over, Tal grabbed the sleeve of my t-shirt and pulled me towards a big building which turned out to be a coffee bar. 'Brân is old Welsh for raven,' Tal explained excitedly. 'It's not ravens who protect the country, it's Raven. Brân!'

As we queued up I told him about the well under the bench with the money in it, but he wasn't really listening. We got a diet Coke each and a ham salad roll to share. Tal was jiggling his way along the queue as though he was going to burst with frustration.

'I told you!' Tal said, unscrewing the Coke cap. 'All this business about the Crown Jewels – I mean – what's the point of having all this security for that? They could just put them in a vault in the Bank of England. And why are the Yeomen ex-Forces? Because they are protecting the

204

Head that's protecting the country, that's why.'

I cut the bread roll in two and offered the plate.

Tal looked at the two pieces carefully, hovering his hand over each in turn. 'This one's got more lettuce.'

He gave that half to me, but I didn't care because I was thinking about what Tal had just said. 'If the security is because of the Head, there's no way we're going to be able to take it from here to a safe place, is there? But if we can't get it, Sian Llewelyn can't, either. Which means it's safe.'

Tal picked up his Coke bottle and shook it. He stared at the explosion of brown bubbles. He didn't agree. 'But Ava, we know it's not safe because – because – Idrys told us.'

We argued about it for a bit longer, and then we ate.

When we finished, we put our rubbish in the bin and went back outside in the sunshine.

'Let's go into the Jewel House,' Tal said. 'That's where it will be if my theory is right. We can work out our plan for getting it out.'

We crossed to the Jewel House and queued again. The doors were really thick and made of metal, and there was a Yeoman Warder standing guard outside. I didn't think we had any chance of smuggling anything out. Inside there were more Yeomen Warders and as we shuffled along with the crowd, half-watching a film of the coronation, Tal ducked under a red rope.

'Hey! You! No queue-jumping!'

It was worse than school! Tal ducked back to join me, and he started to watch the film as well. The Queen was walking down the aisle in Westminster Abbey in the olden days when she was really young.

When we reached the room with the jewels in, we had to stand on a travelator which took us slowly past the crowns. The jewels glittered and winked in glass cases and the labels said things like, five hundred carats of gems.

'It's just crowns,' Tal said in disgust.

'They're not going to put a skull on display,' I said logically.

'That's true. It'll be in an ossuary,' Tal said. 'That's what they call them. It's a box for bones.'

'I know,' I said. 'For the bones of a saint.' When I went to St. Winifred's well with Nain, it was some special day for the sick. There were lots of people there in wheelchairs, and we kissed St. Winifred's bones which were in a little box, even though we weren't Catholics, or sick - Nain said St. Winifred wouldn't mind. Then we rolled up our trousers and walked into the well, which was like a paddling pool, and Nain said her knees felt a lot better afterwards. 'You'd think a holy relic would be in a church or something,' I said to Tal. We were back outside now, blinking in the sunlight after the dark and gloomy Jewel House. I looked across at the White Tower; it was tall and square and imposing against the blue sky, but it wasn't white. I had an idea. 'Where's the map? You should look on the map for a church.'

On the green lawn, the ravens were preening their glossy feathers. We leant against the ancient Roman wall at the side of the White Tower. Tal took the map out of his pocket and flattened it out on his knee. I looked at it over his shoulder.

'There's a chapel here, in the White Tower, the Chapel of St. John the Evangelist,' he said, turning to look. 'See? Where that big curve is? It's different from the other corners of the Tower.'

I started to feel hopeful. 'Did the Triad say anything about a chapel?'

'Er – "The Head of Brân the Blessed, son of Llyr, which was concealed in the White Hill in London, with its face towards France. And as long as it was in the position it was put there, no disaster would ever come to this Island."' Tal took the compass out of his bag and we watched the needle swing. The chapel faced south-east.

Ah-ha!

To get to the entrance, we had to climb up the wooden steps on the outside of the building. Down beneath us, the black ravens croaked.

Tal was studying the map again. 'If we go up the Great Staircase,' he said, 'we'll be on the right floor.'

The Staircase was spiral and narrow. Doors led off it, blocked by red rope.

I followed Tal, and suddenly we were in the small Chapel. It was made of some sort of pale stone, all of it, even the altar. The thick glass windows let in a milky light.

There wasn't much in the chapel to look at. The pale stone pillars were very plain and simple, with no decoration apart from a brass cross. There were no graves or memorials.

I thought about St. Winifred. 'If it's anywhere,' I said to Tal, 'it will be by the altar. Go and look, and I'll keep an eye out for the guards.'

'You go.'

'I'm not looking for a skull. I'm squeamish.'

We argued about it for a minute and then I couldn't stand it any longer. I ducked under the red rope, waiting to get stopped at any moment.

I always feel as if people are watching me, even if they're not. Then I felt indignant. So what if I'd gone under the rope? I could be really religious, I thought, and I could desperately need to go to by the altar to say my prayers. I shut my eyes and prayed I would find the Head. Then I crossed myself and nipped behind the altar. Suddenly, Tal was there too, crouching next to me. As we hid, I stared at the base of it.

The altar was made of the same stone as the pillars. But right at the bottom, there was a square stone with worn carving on it. I knelt on the floor, tracing the words with my finger. Disappointingly, it didn't read like Head or Brân. 'B-E-N'

'Ben?'

'-D-I-G-E-I-D-U-R-A-N – '

'Bendigeiduran, mab Llyr!' he whispered excitedly. 'Blessed Brân, son of Llyr!'

We stared at each other, wide-eyed. We'd found it!!! Our troubles were over!!!

That's what we thought, anyway.

The truth was, they were only just beginning.

Chapter Twenty-One

I held my breath as he lifted the slab of stone. For a moment I thought of worms and maggots. What if the Head was rotten? Then I remembered that the Head was ancient and a skull. The flesh had rotted a long time ago.

Tal peered through the hole.

'Can you see anything?'

'Yes, I think so. But it's sacred. Should we touch it?'

'We'll have to, to get it out.' The blood was whooshing so hard in my ears that it sounded like the sea. I don't like dead things. I wouldn't even touch my hamster after it died, and I'd had him two years.

'Here goes,' Tal said. 'I'll hold the stone and you grab the Head.'

I stuck my hand inside and my fingers and thumb wedged in the eye sockets, like a bowling ball. And I brought the skull out into the light.

Tal's eyes shone and he held his hands out, afraid to touch it.

211

'Okay,' I said. I put it in the backpack. Then Tal put the heavy stone back in place.

We stared at each other in triumph! We'd done it!

Then we checked the other end of the chapel. Tal went first, and when he got over the rope barrier he waved at me to hurry up, but, just my luck, a Yeoman Warder had seen me. He didn't look happy. He folded his arms across his red tunic and waited for me.

'See this?' he asked, pointing to the red rope. 'This means Keep Out.'

'Ach,' I said, slapping myself and pretending I was German. 'Zo sorry.'

He unhooked it and let me out.

I hoped I wouldn't get struck by lightning for lying to a Yeoman Warder in a chapel. 'Don't say anything,' I whispered to Tal, trying not to jump up and down with happiness, 'but I can feel it in the bag. It feels really powerful.' The skull hadn't seemed heavy when I took it out of the ossuary, but I could feel it pressing against my shoulder blades. It felt hot.

We followed the flow of people to a display case with Henry the Eighth's suit of armour. I tried to see what they were looking at but Tal punched me on my arm. 'Come on. Let's get out of here.'

We hurried down the Great Staircase towards the exit, which was in the basement of the White Tower. There were cannons there, and models of the way the Tower had looked throughout the ages. The largest display case backed up against a semi-circular wall which meant we were right beneath the chapel.

As we walked into the gift shop we passed a large stone well in the middle of it.

What is it about wells? I always have to look into them to see how far down the water is. This one was deep and the water was black with the gift shop lights reflected in it. There were hand and footholds jutting out of the brickwork inside but I couldn't imagine why anyone would want to climb in.

I found a pound coin in my jeans, dropped it in and shut my eyes. But before I could make my wish, Tal said,

'Come on,' and pulled me past it.

I glanced longingly at the souvenirs. But I had a stolen skull in my bag, I realised nervously and you couldn't get a bigger souvenir than that. We came out of the shop opposite the Waterloo Block, where the Crown Jewels were.

It had started to rain hard and people were hurrying inside to keep dry.

'Right,' Tal said, 'we've got three exits to choose from. The main exit will be busier but if it's busy, maybe they won't search us.'

So we dashed through the rain. I'd done enough queuing to last me for ages! But it wasn't busy. Everyone was sheltering inside, except for the three Yeomen Warders whose job it was to search the bags.

'I've got a bad feeling about this. Let's try the other exit,' Tal said, stretching his neck. 'The one near Traitor's Gate.'

We retraced our steps. I was nervous again now. Suddenly I saw the German family who had been in the queue as we came in. They had their souvenir umbrellas up. 'Let's tag along,' I said, putting Tal's bag back on my shoulder, and we shuffled along in the rain behind

214

them, trying to look as though we belonged.

We walked past Henry III's Watergate, and there was only one Yeoman standing guard by the exit, wearing the uniform with the black and red hat. Straight in front of us we could see the Wharf and the River Thames and Tower Bridge - we were so close to doing everything that Idrys had asked us to do!

The Yeoman Warder started checking the German family. They were asking him about the Territorial Army's Fly Past the following day and it seemed to take an age. But finally he let the parents go through and Tal and I shuffled a few steps closer to freedom.

Suddenly a man pushed in front of us. For a moment all I saw was a wet brown pony tail trailing over his shoulder. He smiled immediately, as if he'd been waiting for us for a long time and he was happy we'd finally arrived.

'Hello, young lady,' Gwilliam Johnson said, blocking my way. 'How is the school project coming along?'

Chapter Twenty-Two

I was too surprised to answer.

Gwilliam gripped his arms around our necks and turned us around the way we came, past the Watergate, back under the arch to the Tower Green. The rain was lashing down, plastering my hair to my cheeks.

Gwilliam squinted at the White Tower. 'Those bricked-up windows are the windows that Sian's ancestor Gruffudd ap Llewelyn fell from when Henry III imprisoned him. He was trying to escape down knotted bed sheets. Plucky race, the Welsh. Good fighters. Fearless, you might say. And the Wall Walk Towers have some graffiti written by our old friend Garnet. Very clever of you to engage me in that way, Ava.' He hummed cheerfully to himself for a moment. Then he said, 'What's in the backpack?'

'Nothing. We haven't done our shopping yet.'

'Ah,' Gwilliam said, 'you lie so well I almost believe you.'

'What do you want the Head for anyway?' Tal asked. 'I thought you liked old books.'

Gwilliam laughed as if it was the funniest thing he'd heard all day. 'Correction, my dear boy. I like money. I'm going to sell it.'

'But what about the country?' Tal asked fiercely.

'That, dear boy, is just a legend invented by primitive minds. However, if it bothers you that much, I'll sell it back to our own dear government. Or will I? It all depends on who offers the highest bid.' He stared at the Tower through the dripping rain. 'Ah,' he said happily, 'the deaths this place has seen!'

In a flash, I imagined the future. Yeoman Warders would take people round Tower Green and say that this was where two young friends had been killed after they stole the Head of the Blessed Brân. We'd be history. My dad would have my name put on a bench.

'How did you know the Head was here?' Tal asked.

'Because I followed you. I eventually realised, as you did, that Idrys wouldn't have had a book at all. It was all supposed to be remembered. And with his memory gone, the latest edition of the Druid's Book, let us call it, was you. So I closed the shop and drove to London. Ava had trustingly given me her address, which made it ridiculously easy for me to find you.'

As we came out from under the shadow of the arch, the rain hit us like cold needles. I looked to the left, towards the bench where the half-moon well was, and I thought of all the money that I'd never collected and maybe never would.

Tower Green was empty. Even the ravens were sheltering from the weather.

Gwilliam led us into the shadow of the walls. 'Give me the bag,' he said.

Without his wigs he was a lot more scary so I slipped the bag off my shoulders.

'Open it,' he commanded.

My hands were shaking but I unzipped it and he took it from me and looked inside.

Then he took the skull out. It was yellowy-brown with age and the teeth grinned.

Gwilliam turned it over in his hands and looked at it carefully. He smiled. 'Marvellous,' he murmured. 'Do you know how much this is worth? As a Christian relic, as the saint who brought Christianity to these shores, this skull is worth a fortune.' He glanced at us happily. 'Do you know what I'm going to do with the money? I'm going to retire to Goa. Do you know Goa? No? Ah, well.' His smile faded. 'But first, we've got to get it out of here,' Gwilliam said to me, 'and this is where you come in. Tie it to your belt,' he said to me. 'Luckily you're a plump girl and it won't look too noticeable if you pull your t-shirt over it.'

Plump? Cheek! I unbuckled my belt and threaded it through the eye sockets. 'I'm going to tell Dad you've stolen the Head, by the way,' I warned him, just to let him know he couldn't get away with it.

'But, my dear, who stole it first? You,' he said to Tal, 'can carry the bag. Let them search it. And don't try to alert anyone. Do you know the trouble you'll be in for stealing this particular treasure? It's a terrorist act and no-one likes terrorists, do they?'

I put the belt around my waist, pulling my baggy t-shirt down to hide the skull. 'The well's over there,' I whispered to Tal. 'We can jump in and swim to safety!'

'And drown, you mean,' Tal whispered, putting his arms through the backpack.

'We won't drown. The well's deep and the water comes from the river. At least we'd have a chance.'

'I won't. I can't swim.'

'What? Everyone can swim!' But I could see by his tight face he was telling the truth. That's what happens when you don't go to school - you miss the interesting bits, too. 'Don't worry, I'm a brilliant swimmer and I'll hang onto you. It's by that bench, see? Jump in after me, okay?'

He nodded, and we started to run back along the path that led to a dead end.

Gwilliam turned and laughed at us.

Who cared? We were going to escape!

But when I pushed the bench aside and we looked down at the black water, it suddenly seemed a very bad idea indeed.

Gwilliam was coming briskly towards us with a vicious grin on his face.

I clutched Tal's hand.

We jumped into the well together.

Chapter Twenty-Three

We hit the cold water in a flurry of bubbles.

Tal sank like a rock, like a deadweight, pulling me down down down until my ears popped with the pressure. I pinched my nose with my free hand and swallowed.

In the blurry gloom I saw two small dark tunnels leading out of the stone well. The current tugged us, and gripping Tal's fingers, I eased into the bigger tunnel, pulling him behind me. His backpack was getting in the way, and wedging my feet against the walls, I took it off Tal's shoulders. His eyes were huge and terrified, and I did a thumbs-up, clutched his hand again and started swimming. The tunnel was so narrow it was hard for us to keep hold of each other. Slimy moss and weed slithered over our faces as we kicked our way through the murky water.

After a couple of minutes, I was desperate for air and really scared. The blood was thumping behind my eyes in a red ache. My arms were tired and my chest hurt - the tunnel was pitch black and impossibly long. Surely we should be at the river by now?

I kicked harder, but Tal dragged behind. His fingers were loosening from mine, letting go. He had stopped kicking. Suddenly, the water in the tunnel was still.

I turned around in the narrow space, needing to breathe, and I tried to find him in the slippery dark. It was hopeless. We were going to die after all. We were going to drown. And we'd never be found. Dad would be looking for me for the rest of his life.

In despair, I breathed out my last bubble of air and as I watched it rise, silver and wobbly like mercury, I breathed in water, I couldn't help it. I felt my throat tighten and I saw there was a light glowing in the tunnel with us. It was warm and yellow, like sunlight rippling on sand. In the mud I could see jewelled swords twinkling and glowing, and coins, and golden bowls half-filled with mud. I trailed my hands over them. Treasure! I smiled, and swallowed water, but I didn't choke. I felt dreamy, happy, breathing in the golden underwater light. And then I floated right over Tal. He was lying face up, staring, but he couldn't see me. His dead eyes were white and blank, like plastic.

I caught hold of his black t-shirt and his arms moved towards me for a moment, but then he sank down again and settled on the silt.

And then I realised that the light wasn't sunlight - it was coming from the skull tied to my belt. I put my hands on the Head, catching my thumb on the jagged nose, and a burst of energy shot through me as if I'd been drinking Red Bull.

I pulled Tal up and tucked my hands under his armpits, lying on my back like a life-saver. The skull was between us and I started kicking, counting as I went, one-two-three-four, two-two-three-four, three-two-three-four. I could see a cold light in the distance. Four-two-three-four, five-two-three–

And suddenly we were out of the tunnel and floundering in the wide grey water of the Thames. I held onto Tal, gasping for breath under the dark wet sky. On our right was Tower Bridge, painted blue. I could see people on it hurrying past under umbrellas, cars driving across, but no-one saw us, no-one even looked. In the middle of the city, it seemed like Tal and I were the only two people in the world. My feet touched the river bed and I held his face above the water and looked around at the Tower. It was low tide. In front of us was the river wall and a small beach, with pebbles and brown sand, and I dragged Tal out of the Thames and crouched next to him on my hands and knees, burping up water and dry-heaving as though my insides were going to split. I wiped my mouth on my arm and bent over him. His face was pale and eyes were still staring at nothing and I knew he was dead.

It was my fault. He'd told me he couldn't swim, hadn't he? And I'd told him it would be all right. I'd promised to hang onto him, so he'd trusted me. Well, I had hung onto him, hadn't I? But it hadn't done him any good.

The tears were hot on my cheeks. I tried to imagine him meeting up with Idrys in the Otherworld, but I couldn't. Instead I got so angry that it seemed to burst out of me like a volcano. I hated the Head of Brân more than I'd ever hated anything in my life before. I unfastened my belt and took the skull off it and hit Tal on the chest with it.

'Stupid skull! Stupid, stupid bloody skull! It's all your fault!'

A deep croaky voice said, 'Stoooop yelllling.'

It scared the life out of me - I thought the skull was talking.

Then Tal hurled. Water came gushing out of him in huge spurts like a Super Soaker and finally he gave a cough and vomited a pale lump of ham roll down his t-shirt. He sat up, holding the skull. 'That's better,' he said hoarsely.

I pulled a face. The sick was steaming in the rain. 'It's all over you, Tal.'

'Yes,' he grinned weakly, 'but at least it's warm.'

I started to laugh with relief, and I flopped weakly back on the pebbles and felt the rain on my face and Tal laughed, too. A silver aeroplane slid slowly out of the dark clouds and I felt really happy. We were amazingly still alive.

But we were also wet and cold.

We wanted to go home.

I felt my pockets. My money was soaking and sticking together. 'Oops.'

Tal took his leather wallet out of his pocket and took out some wet notes. 'Mine's gone brown.'

'I don't know if a taxi will take us for wet money.' We looked at each other. 'I could ring my Dad to pick us up,' I said.

'What will he say?'

I wasn't sure. I didn't like to think about it. Something that involved telling me off, that kind of thing. Then I had another thought. 'Or Caroline, then. She lives in Bermondsey.' As soon as I said her name, it seemed a good idea.

We walked along the shingle, shaking and shivering, until we came to some steps. A boy and girl were sitting under a striped umbrella with their arms around each other, smoking.

When the boy saw us, he was so surprised he dropped his cigarette between his legs and leapt up quickly in case his jeans caught fire.

'Been swimming?' he asked when he'd got his cigarette back. His girlfriend laughed.

'We fell in,' I said.

'Cool,' the girl said, blowing smoke towards the sky.

'Have you got a phone we could borrow? I've got to ring my –' I stopped. I was going to say, my dad's girlfriend, but I changed it to '- my mum.' It seemed more serious, somehow.

'We can pay you,' Tal offered, tucking the skull under his arm, 'only the money's a bit wet.' He handed over a brown fiver.

'No, don't worry,' the girl said, so I rang Caroline and asked her to pick us up from Tower Bridge and to bring some towels because we'd got a bit wet. She said she would see us in ten minutes.

We thanked the couple and went up the steps. Tal was still holding the skull. When I'd first met him, I'd thought he was a Goth. Now he really looked like one.

We stood on the bridge and watched a police helicopter fly over. It hovered above the Tower, and then it was joined by another one.

After a few minutes a car tooted us, and Caroline flung the door open. She was all in red. 'Quick!' she yelled, 'I'm not supposed to park here! Sit on the towels or you'll rot the leather!'

We jumped into the back seat and sat on the white towels as she pulled away with a screech. By the lights, she turned round to look us up and down, pursing her red lips.

I waited for her to yell at us or something, but she didn't.

She said, 'You want to go to mine and get dry?'

'Yes, please,' we said together.

'Okay,' she said, and switched the radio on.

We listened to music as she drove back to her flat.

I'd been to her flat once before, and I liked it. It was modern and new.

We stood shivering in the kitchen while Caroline made three black coffees, and then she said, 'Tal, you can shower in the en-suite, and Ava, you can take a bath in there. Leave your clothes outside the door. Do you want to ring your dad? Tell him I'll drop you off.'

So I rang him and said we'd been to the Tower of London on an educational visit and we'd got caught in the rain. Which was true.

Then I went into Caroline's bathroom with a black coffee and the skull. She had a lot of Cowshed products lined up on a dark wooden shelf. I squirted Dirty Cow into the bath and turned the taps full on, and left my clothes outside the door as she'd told me to.

I put the skull by the taps so that I could look at it, and I got into the bath. It was hot and frothy - it was like lying in latte.

The skull wasn't glowing. It was just a skull, propped up on a bath.

But…

It had lit up a tunnel and showed me gold and jewels, and it had given me energy to swim and it had brought Tal back from the dead.

The row of teeth grinned.

I suddenly imagined my mum wearing a yellow hard hat and a big smile in Nepal, surrounded by children. I could bring her home. I could heal Nain with it.

And I could be a swimming champion, because in the tunnel, after the skull had glowed, I'd been jet-propelled.

I watched the skull through the steam. But it wasn't a skull – it looked like a face, with skin and, I saw with surprise, eyes in the empty sockets. Brown eyes. Brown hair, too. Long. And a brown moustache.

The teeth were the same. He was still smiling. I knew why Sian Llewelyn wanted the Head so badly. With that Head, a person could do anything...

The bubbles were bursting around my chin like little kisses and I opened my eyes. I felt tired but really happy, and I wrapped myself up in Caroline's dressing gown and went back into the lounge. Tal was dressed, and his face looked shiny.

Caroline gave us our clothes back. They still smelled of well water and sick but they were warm from the tumble dryer. And they were dry.

When we got home, Dad opened the door and looked at Tal, dressed in black, carrying a skull.

'Alas, poor Yorick,' he said, and grinned. 'Hello Caroline. Glass of wine?'

'Super.'

I walked past the fish tank.

Tal and I looked at the fake skull in the tank and then at the real skull. We had to hide it in a safe place. Somewhere no-one would think of looking. The trouble was, it was impossible to think of a place that no-one would think of looking. Because as soon as we thought of one, we knew they'd think of it, too. I had an idea. 'We could put it in the tank,' I said to Tal, 'and swap it, so that people will think it's the old fake one.'

'No,' Tal said, 'it's too obvious. We need somewhere really safe, because one thing's for sure, they're all going to come looking for it. A safe! Has your Dad got a safe?'

'No. We don't have anything valuable enough.' Then I had an idea. 'My mum's left some hats behind. We could put a hat on it! Pretend it's a hat stand!'

Tal screwed up his nose. 'Definitely not.'

'My bedside drawer!'

'That's the first place they'll look.'

'Under my pillow! In the oven? The washing machine? The linen basket? The freezer?' I was just starting to go mad when Dad came hurrying in, his face pink with happiness.

'Caroline's staying for supper,' he said. 'What food did you get?'

Uh-oh.

'Anything that will spoil?'

'No,' Tal and I said together.

'Good. Let's get pizza.' He was already dialling. 'Pull out the table, will you. And we'll have chicken wings, and dough balls. Hello? Yes, Gino. Yes, this is Mike Jones. We'll have a Mega Pepperoni…'

'With salad!' Caroline called.

We always ask him for the same things.

I went into the kitchen to pull out the table. It's a Danish table, circular, and you twist it underneath, and the leaves disengage, and from the hole in the centre you can pull out three more leaves out of the hole to make the table bigger.

Tal watched me for a moment. Then he said, 'Ava – we should put the Head in there.'

I still liked the fish tank idea best so I could look at it whenever I wanted to. But the important thing was to keep it safe. I shrugged. 'Okay.'

'Then,' Tal said, 'we could lay the table and just keep a cloth on it all the time. No-one will think of looking inside a table. And Ava – wrap it in a cloth out of respect.'

I fetched a pillowcase and we put the Head on it and then we both sat down and looked at it for a few minutes. It was strange – it didn't seem the slightest bit creepy to be sitting by the table with a real skull. In fact, it gave me a good, warm feeling which was hard to explain. 'It's as if we know him,' I said.

Tal nodded. 'Yeah. Triad Ninety-Three. "And it was not more irksome to them having the Head with them, than if Bendigeid Fran had been with them himself."'

'Exactly! For a skull, he's good company.'

'And he's quiet. Not like Gwilliam.'

'Yeah, not like Gwilliam.'

Tal wrapped it up carefully and put it inside the table. We closed the extra leaves, and I put a white tablecloth on it.

As I set out the cutlery, I asked a question that been worrying me. We'd saved the skull from destruction – but what about that fiery scene in Nain's glasses that I'd seen? Was it still going to take place? 'Tal, what's going to happen now?'

Tal bit the edge of his thumb. He looked at me briefly, and then he looked away. I got the feeling that it was something he'd been wondering about, too.

'It doesn't really matter what happens,' he said after a moment. 'That's nothing to do with us. The important thing is, we've done what Idrys asked. We've protected the Head of Brân. We've done our bit.'

'Yes, you're right,' I agreed, but deep down I wasn't sure it was as simple as that.

Chapter Twenty-Four

Early next morning, I woke up feeling as excited as Christmas. Then I remembered about the Head that was secretly hidden in our table.

I got dressed and hurried downstairs. Dad had left for work, and he'd finished off the pizza from last night. There was a note propped on the table:

FOOD?

I got the Head out of the hole in the table and put it in my sports bag. I laid the table again as quietly as I could because I didn't want to wake Tal. I knew for a fact that he wasn't going to approve of what I was going to do next: I was taking it to show Nain.

She'd done a really brave thing getting Idrys out of Whitehill, even though it meant acting crazy herself and I wanted her to hold it in the hope it would make her feet better. I peered through the front window, just in case someone was watching.

Sure enough, Gwilliam was sitting outside in our street in his little black car.

It was totally steamed up, so he'd probably been there for quite a while. He'd slid the window down to save from suffocating and as I watched him he started picking his nose out of boredom. Disgusting.

I left through the back door, cut through the garden and scrambled over our neighbour's fence. This is more dangerous than it sounds, because he's not keen on children, not even me. His garden's really neat, except for the bit of fence which belongs to his neighbour on the other side, and I struggled over the broken section, went through the back garden of the other neighbour, tip-toed past the back door and came out in the next street up from ours. When I reached the top of the estate I ran along Hampstead Lane all the way to the The Woodlands Care Home. It was just off Bishop's Avenue and it was modern, with so much glass that it looked like a school.

At reception, a woman in a blue uniform took me to see her. Nain wasn't playing bridge with the white-haired, handsome old man in the picture on the web site – she was sitting amongst large potted ferns, reading the newspapers in a bamboo chair in the conservatory with her feet on a stool. She was wearing a trendy new pair of glasses with red frames.

'Ava!' she said, putting the papers down as she saw me. 'No school today?'

'It's still the summer holidays,' I said, sitting on the edge of the stool.

'Goodness me, you do have a long time,' she said disapprovingly.

Not long enough, as far as I'm concerned, but I decided not to argue because I had the sports bag on my knee. 'Nain, you know when we went to St. Winifred's Well and your knees got better?' I unzipped the bag and put the Head in her hands.

'Heavens! What's this?'

'Don't drop it! It's the Head of Brân.'

'Bendigeid Frân?' Nain looked at it in awe. She studied it carefully, as though she was checking it for damage. She curved her hand around the smooth bone and then she looked at me suspiciously. 'What are you doing with it? You haven't stolen it, have you?'

I don't know what it is, but grandparents always think the worst. 'No. Hold it tight and you'll feel better.'

238

Nain's bony fingers moved gently across the dome of the skull, and around the cheekbones. She started to smile. 'I imagine he had soft hair,' she said. 'Dark, too. The Celts always were dark. No beard, I think – fancy! I always imagined the old druids as bearded.'

'Do you feel different yet?'

She thought about it for a moment, and then she looked at me over her glasses. 'Ava, it's always relaxing to have someone's Head in your lap.'

Spooky!

I watched her and fidgeted because I was impatient for something good to happen. 'How do your feet feel?'

She looked at them curiously and wriggled her toes. 'They feel very comfortable,' she said.

Comfortable is Nain-speak for fine, so I was pleased. 'Do you want to go for a little walk?'

'Well,' she said, 'I could try, but not too far.'

I helped her out of the chair while she shouted orders at me.

'Hold my elbow! No, not my arm – my elbow! Not that one, this one!' she said as

I ran around her. 'Wait! Wait!' After a lot of wobbling, she was standing upright. Well, not exactly upright – she was a bit bent and her bottom was sticking out, but it was a good try.

Then she started to walk in a shuffle, and I jumped around her to catch her in case she fell.

'Out of the way! Out of the way!' she shouted urgently, as if she was going to run me over. She didn't stop until she reached the palm tree in the pot. 'Turn me round!' she said.

So I did, and then she shuffled back to the chair, turned around by herself, and sat down breathlessly, patting her chest. When she'd stopped panting, she said, 'I'm very pleased about that. What a blessing,' she said, 'to be in the company of the Wondrous Head.' She looked at me over her new glasses. 'But one thing bothers me, Ava. What are you doing with it?'

'Well,' I explained, feeling really happy with myself, 'Idrys told us to protect it so that it didn't get destroyed. So we're hiding it from Sian Llewelyn and Gwilliam Johnson and James, because they all want it for themselves and Gwilliam says it's worth a fortune.'

Modestly I waited for her to say how clever we were, but she didn't.

She frowned. 'Idrys told you to protect it so that it wouldn't be destroyed but he didn't mean you to move it.' She looked very serious, and she took her trendy red glasses off and looked at me through her watery blue eyes. 'I seem to remember King Arthur moved it once,' she said, 'because he wanted all the credit for keeping the country safe. And look what happened! Years of war and conflict! His son, smarter than him but with less of a reputation for it, had to put it back in the end.'

'But Idrys said – '

'Idrys! Idrys wanted you to look after it! And here you are, walking around the streets with it in a bag as if you own it!'

I hate it when she's angry. 'But I wanted to help you!' I protested, and my eyes filled with tears. Sometimes I can't do anything right.

'Come here,' she said, holding her arms out. She sat me down and kissed me and cupped her warm hands around my face, smeared my tears with her thumbs.

'You have helped me. But you have to put it back, you know that, don't you? You have to put it back where it belongs.'

'But I can't!'

'Listen to me,' she said. 'Something bad is going to happen, you know that, don't you?'

My heart jumped. 'Yes! But what, exactly?'

'I wish I knew.'

'Can we stop it?'

'Can you stop it?' She laughed, surprised that I'd asked. 'No, of course you can't. But you can influence the outcome.'

'How?'

'I can't do your thinking for you. Use your God-given wits. Go now. Put the Head back where it belongs. I wish I could help you,' she said, putting her glasses back on. 'I will pray for you.' She grasped my hand and squeezed it tightly. 'Be careful, Ava, won't you?'

I nodded dismally. I thought about the Yeomen warders and the long, long dark tunnel and I just wanted it all to be over.

Nain looked worried, too. 'Be very careful,' she repeated, as though she knew more than she was telling.

I looked quickly at the glasses, scared I was going to see my own dead body reflected back, but all I could see in them were her watery eyes, magnified by the lenses, full of love.

I was just creeping carefully back through the neighbour's garden, the one who doesn't like children, when I heard some yelling coming from my house. I scrambled over the fence and as I opened the back door I saw Tal and Rosie running out through the front door, yelling at the tops of their voices.

'Hey!' I shouted, and slid on the wet hall floor. What the - ?

A car engine fired up in the street. I reached the front gate just in time to see Tal chasing James, and Gwilliam driving after them both at top speed. He hit the car roof with a jolt as he went over the speed bumps.

'What's going on?'

Rosie looked at me, her eyes wide with astonishment. 'James stole your fish-tank ornament!'

'What???' Things were happening that would sound totally senile if I wasn't seeing them for myself. Down the avenue, James body swerved away from Tal and pushed open the communal door of the block of flats just as Gwilliam double-parked, blocking the road. He jumped out of the car and followed James into the flats.

Tal raced back along the road towards us. 'Where's the Head?' he asked me. 'It's not in the table.'

'It's here.' I patted it.

'James came round – '

'And he swore he didn't know anything about Gwilliam – '

'And then he stuck his hand in your fish tank and ran away!'

I looked at my watch. It was still only just turned ten and already bad things were happening. I'd only been gone an hour!

'He'll soon find out it's not the right skull,' I said. 'It's got Made in China underneath it.'

We were standing on the pavement, staring at the block of flats to see what would happen next.

Moments later Gwilliam came dashing out holding something under his jacket.

He jumped into his car just as James came out, and then he reversed at high speed and turned down the hill where he turned right at Tesco, burning rubber, and disappeared from view.

James heard us laughing.

He looked at us over his shoulder and pushed his dark hair out of his eyes with his arm.

He looked so lonely standing there that it just didn't seem funny anymore and I started to feel sorry for him all over again.

'Shall I go and tell him it's not the real Head?'

'No!!!!' Rosie and Tal said together.

So we went back into the house and locked the doors, just in case.

In the lounge my fish were swimming around wondering where their house had vanished to and what on earth had happened.

We sat around the kitchen table and I broke the bad news about what Nain had said about the Head. 'She says we've got to take it back into the Tower.'

'That's stupid,' Tal said. 'That's dumb – that's crazy! We can't. What if it's destroyed?'

'That's exactly what I thought! But Nain says it has to stay in the Tower no matter what because the last time it was moved there were years of wars or something.' History's not my best subject.

'But Idrys said -'

'He didn't tell us to move it, did he?'

I could see Tal going through the conversation in his mind. He chewed the edge of his thumbnail. 'No. He didn't tell us to do that.'

Rosie slammed her hand on the table in frustration. 'I don't understand! Who wants to destroy it? How? Where? And why?'

Tal and I looked each other.

'Gwilliam wouldn't destroy it – he wants to sell it.'

'Sian's senile enough,' I said.

'She's not senile. She's too young.'

'Senile means –' I tapped my temple – 'crazy.'

'It means old.'

My face got hot. Thanks a lot, Nain, I thought.

I stared at the ceiling and tried to think. 'We need another druid to help us,' I said, 'someone who understands.' I had a sudden inspiration. 'Someone high up! And who's not dead. Like the ex-Archbishop of Canterbury! We could ring him – how can we get his number?'

'From Lambeth Palace,' Tal said.

So I Googled the number of Lambeth Palace and then I rang it. I thought the phrase 'druid terrorism' would work, because it sounded serious. But no. 'They hung up,' I said.

I sat down at the kitchen table, feeling hopeless. We were on our own and I'd run out of ideas. We knew something bad was going to happen. We knew that we had to go back to The Tower and both of these facts scared me so much I felt sick.

'So now what?'

'Nain said we have to use our God-given wits.'

We looked at each other hopefully for signs of wits.

'That's easy for her to say,' Tal said after a moment.

'I wonder where James is now?' Rosie asked.

'Looking for Gwilliam,' I said.

'Yeah...where's Gwilliam, do you think?'

Tal shrugged. We weren't getting very far.

'There's three of them against three of us,' I said.

'Not exactly,' said Rosie. 'There's the three of us against two of them, plus Gwilliam.' Her maths was coming in useful already,

'Okay,' Tal said. 'That's a good way of looking at it, Rosie.'

Not that I was jealous or anything but I said, 'She thinks you're a geek, by the way.'

Tal ignored me. 'Let's start with the facts. They don't know that we've still got the real skull so at this moment, we're safe. Secondly, the last place they'll expect us to take it is back to the Tower, right? So we've got no time to lose. We'll take the Head back right now, but this time, Ava, I will swim through the tunnel.'

I looked up at him in astonishment. 'Tal, you can't swim.'

'I think I was getting the hang of it towards the end.'

I snorted. 'No you weren't. You actually drowned.'

'I'd do it,' Rosie said, 'but I don't like getting my hair wet.'

'It's true,' I told Tal. 'Her hair goes all frizzy. Look, I'll do it, but this time I'll be prepared. I need a snorkel, flippers, goggles and my swimsuit. Hey - remember the well in the gift shop,' I said, thinking about it, 'in the basement of the White Tower?'

'You threw a pound in.'

'Yeah, and I bet the two wells join up. If I swim straight through, and come up in the White Tower gift shop, I could use the hand and foot-holds to climb out.'

'We'll get caught,' Rosie said nervously.

'No, we won't,' Tal said. 'Because at two o'clock this afternoon, everyone will be outside watching the Territorial Army Fly Past.'

'Genius!' I'd forgotten all about that.

'And then we'll go up those steps inside the gift shop which lead to the chapel and we'll put the Head back.'

Simple!

My kit was in the shed. Rosie and I collected everything together in double-quick time and I practised breathing through the snorkel while we worked out the plan in the kitchen.

We were all going to leave for the Tower at the same time, with a decoy sports bag each. Tal was going to run to the tube, Rosie was catching the bus and I was going to cycle along the back streets to confuse them.

'So,' Tal said, 'you'll climb up the well and we'll wait for you –'

'– and help you out,' Rosie finished.

'And bring my extra clothes for me to wear,' I told her, 'because I'll have to leave mine by the river.' I wasn't going to walk about in public in my swimsuit.

I put my cozzie on and got dressed in my oldest shorts.

Back in the kitchen we put the Head on the table for the last time and we put our hands on it, like baseball players. It was cool and smooth.

'Okay, well, here we go. Good luck everyone,' Tal said, and he took a deep breath.

'Good luck.'

He put the Head back in my sports bag.

'I just wish it was over and done with,' Rosie said.

'Me too.' I was just about to wheel my bike out when the phone rang.

It took me a moment to recognise Nain's agitated voice.

'Sian Llewelyn's just been here,' she said. 'She brought my medical documents for the manager and she tried to find out about the Head of Brân! The nerve of her! I told her you were taking it back where it belonged.'

I felt my heart lurch with dismay. 'You *told* her? Oh, Nain.'

'Ava.' Tal reached for the phone. His hands cast a shadow in the sunlight. It looked like a raven with its wings outstretched. It looked so real that I could see the breath moving its throat, and the glint of its eye. 'It's time to go,' he said as he put the phone in its base.

Chapter Twenty-Five

We went outside in the sunshine and shut the door.

I had this bad feeling that someone was watching us and Tal did, too. He didn't hang around – he started to run, and I got on my bike. I could hear the bus coming up the hill, which meant that in a minute or two there would be another one coming down.

'See you later,' Rosie said.

I cycled downhill without even keeping my hands on the brakes. Everything seemed different - new – the grass was very green and the flowers were brightly coloured as if I was seeing them for the last time. The wind on my face brought tears to my eyes.

I parked my bike at King's Cross and got a taxi with the educational money. I stared out of the window and thought about the swim.

I knew I had three minutes to reach the half-moon well, where I could take a few deep breaths before the next bit. I wasn't too afraid, because I would have the Head

252

on my belt around my swimsuit and I was pretty sure it would protect me.

I was nervous, though.

I got out of the taxi at Tower Bridge, my heart beating fast, prepared for danger, destruction and maybe death, while people bustled around me, innocently enjoying themselves, thinking about ordinary things and having fun.

I went down the steps to the river. There were a lot of people on the walkway above me and as a helicopter flew by overhead I looked out across the twinkling brown water to the office buildings sparkling in the sun.

I sat on the bottom step and undressed, threading my belt through the Head's eye sockets and fastening it round my waist.

I folded my clothes up neatly and put them into the bag. I put my flippers on and tied my hair back, shivering with nerves, wondering how easy it was going to be to climb out of the well.

I started worrying.

What if something happened when I was inside it?

What if the well caved in? I wouldn't be able to get Blessed Brân back into the

White Tower. Death didn't bother druids, but it certainly bothered me.

'I wish –' Suddenly I had a memory niggling me, and it was something to do with wishing. Yeah – that pound I'd thrown in the well in the gift shop and hadn't made a wish for. I wish I had, now. I would wish it would all work out fine.

I put the snorkel in my mouth. 'Okay,' I said to myself in an echoey voice, 'I'm ready.'

I lowered myself into the cold Thames, adjusting my goggles, looking at the brown floating flecks in the water. And I dived down and started swimming, keeping as close as I could to the embankment wall so that I could judge the speed of the current.

The river was higher and the little beach that Tal and I had lain on was under water which meant I had to dive deeper.

Each time I came up to clear the snorkel I thought that that the next time, I'd find it. Finally, I did, but I had no air left, so I went up to the surface again, tucked the snorkel in my belt, took a few deep breaths and dived straight back down. And I eased myself into the gloomy tunnel.

What I'd remembered about the tunnel was the light shining on the silt, and all that treasure. But this time the Head didn't shine.

I swam in the dark, narrow space, scraping my head on the top of the tunnel, fighting the current. Bubbles flew out of my nose, tickling along my cheeks and neck. My chest was getting tight, but I kept my strokes rhythmic. I started reciting my times tables. One-two-is-two, two-twos-are-four, three-twos -

I touched something bulky and it bobbed up at me. In panic, I pushed it away, swallowing water.

Then I realised with relief what it was. It was Tal's backpack! Four-twos-are-eight, five-twos-are-ten-

I could see light ahead of me.

Seconds later I swam into the well, striking out for the surface, treading water as I breathed in the beautiful air. I could see part of the bench high above me and the black grille over a semi-circle of blue sky.

I let my heart calm down. I could hear the sound of crowds; children laughing, people talking.

Suddenly the sky blacked out and I looked at the sole of someone's trainer. I clung onto the mossy wall and prayed that he wouldn't look down. The visitor moved away and I was looking up at the sky again.

I duck-dived down into the water.

It was shockingly cold.

That's the weird thing about water; you think you've got used to it, and then when you go deep, you're back to square one and freezing again.

I swam into the second passage, the one that led into the White Tower well. It was wider than the first one, and easier to swim through and I reached the gift shop really quickly and looked up at the bright spotlights on the wooden ceiling, expecting, at the rim of the well, to see Rosie.

It was quiet, and every splash echoed loudly.

I took my flippers off and let them float, and pushed the skull around my back so that it wouldn't get scraped as I climbed, moved the goggles onto my forehead and then I reached for the handholds and heaved myself, muscles trembling, out of the water. My arms ached and my own body felt like a dead weight.

I stopped a couple of times as I climbed, but I couldn't hear anything, and no-one came to look, or to throw money in – which was lucky as I didn't feel like being hit on the head with pound coins.

When I reached the rim of the well, two hands reached out to help me. 'Thanks, Rosie!' I said with relief.

I saw the glint of yellow sports goggles and my heart sank.

It wasn't Rosie at all.

It was Sian Llewelyn.

Chapter Twenty-Six

'Gwilliam said you might try swimming through the well,' she said as she dragged me out roughly, nearly pulling my shoulders out of their sockets. I lay in a puddle of water on the stone floor, panting with effort.

Sian tore the packaging from a souvenir jewel-handled letter-opener shaped like a dagger. She watched me clamber to my feet and she pointed it at me.

I looked from the dagger to Sian and back to the dagger again. It looked seriously dangerous for a souvenir. 'Have you paid for that?' I asked suspiciously.

'You are the most irritating girl I have ever met, you know that? I am so tempted to kill you right now. Give me the Head of Brân,' she said, 'and then I'm out of here.'

I fumbled with my belt buckle. 'Where's Rosie?'

'Gwilliam's on baby-sitting duty again. He says he's going to help us get the Head out, but of course we didn't tell him we've already got that sorted.'

'I hope you're a good swimmer.'

'We're not that stupid! We've got a better plan. James is going to create a diversion.'

Uh-oh.

'It's not the bluebottle trick, is it?'

She poked me on the arm. 'Shut up and get a move on. We haven't got all day.'

'I'm doing it as fast as I can!' I protested. 'My hands are shaking!'

I finally got my belt unbuckled, and untethered the Head reluctantly.

She took it with a smile. 'At last,' she said, admiring it for a moment before she put it in her bag.

She adjusted her yellow sports glasses, snapping the rubber strap behind her pony tail. 'Okay, keep walking,' she said.

My wet feet were slipping on the floor as I followed her up the stone steps, through the armoury and past the chapel.

Through the old, thick milky glass that you couldn't really see out of, I could hear the low drone of aircraft overhead.

Sian hurried up the spiral staircase to the entrance, and went out onto the wooden platform at the top of the steps.

There were crowds of people below us, hundreds of them, all looking up at the sky.

'It's not going to be a Successful Enterprise you know,' I said desperately, even though I didn't know how to stop it.

'What?' She turned to look at me, and I saw my reflection in her glasses.

'That pigeon that you killed in the garden at Whitehill. That's disgusting.'

She laughed. 'Yeah, I agree. Animal sacrifice is James's thing,' she said, 'not mine. But hey, he's a good worker and whatever keeps him happy, right?'

From the top of the steps I looked for Rosie and Tal in the crowd. Suddenly I saw Gwilliam Johnson over by the ravens with his arms around their throats, like a fake friendly Dad. They looked desperately miserable and I knew how that felt.

And then I saw James Dodd sneaking round the Roman wall, He was wearing a camouflage jacket that looked a few sizes too big. Successful enterprise, I thought. We should have known it was James who killed the pigeon. There was nothing he enjoyed more than violence and destruction – he'd boasted about it often enough. I wondered what the diversion was going to be. If I could only grab the bag without Sian poking me with the letter-opener -

'Stop fidgeting,' she spat.

'Sorry.'

My eyes went back to Tal standing by the barrier that kept the ravens back. This time he'd seen me, too. He curled his hands against his face as though he was looking through binoculars.

What?

He took his hands away and jerked his head sideways.

I'm hopeless at charades and that kind of thing. What???

I glanced up at Sian. Her yellow glasses were gleaming, and her hair was fluttering in the breeze. She was still looking for James in the crowds.

When I looked back at Tal, he looked different. His fair hair seemed darker; almost black. Gwilliam noticed, too and let him go with the same expression of alarm on his face as Dad that day he saw Idrys in the street. Suddenly free, Tal jumped over the barrier onto the green.

Gwilliam made a grab for him, but it was too late - the ravens rushed at him and Gwilliam kept his distance.

Over the noisy crowd, I heard Tal yell out to me hoarsely. He lifted his arms and they didn't look like arms, they looked like wings, angled and glossy in the shadow of the White Tower.

I tried to find James again. He was still by the old Roman wall in his bulky jacket. He must be sweating in that, I thought. What a weird thing to wear on such a hot day.

Then I looked up, because the sky started to get dark as though there was going to be a storm. Black clouds were gathering so densely that it looked as if there was a blanket over the sky.

But they weren't clouds; they were birds. There were thousands of them swirling above us like swarms of bees. As they flew closer a siren blared. The planes overhead banked and peeled away from the danger.

The bird noise was tremendous and getting louder all the time. My hair was blown by the rush of air from those thousands of beating wings. Tal was standing on the grass of Tower Green, watching them like a huge raven. And around him were the Tower ravens. And above them were hundreds of carrion crows and hooded crows and jackdaws and rooks, tumbling, rolling, gliding and diving like a display team, and the crowds of people were watching in amazement.

Tal was holding his hands behind him, fingers outswept. He called out to me.

'Oh, hell,' Sian said, adjusting her glasses nervously.

With a sweep of wings, a raven took off, soared, and perched on the handrail of the platform; a huge, ugly scavenger.

The birds fluttered and settled and the grass was black with them. They studded the ancient walls in restless rows.

The last time I'd so many black birds was in Nain's glasses.

Suddenly I knew what Tal had been telling me! I knew what I had to do!

Nain had showed me what was going to happen and all I had to do was to help things along. I could change the future!

I grabbed Sian's sports glasses and tried to pull them off so that the birds could peck out her eyes, but she bit me! 'That hurt!' Pain shot through my hand. I'd failed!

'A raven,' Sian sneered. 'Is that the best Tal can do? He should have chosen a real bird.'

She fumbled for the skull and brought it out into the daylight, brandishing it high and raising her face to the sky in triumph. Big mistake.

A low-flying pigeon dropped a big white splat of pigeon poo on her glasses.

'That means good luck,' I said helpfully as she tore them off to clean them.

And something strange started happening.

The multitude of birds rose up in a black cloud and mobbed her in a violent flurry of wings. Sian Llewelyn screamed and covered her head, dropping the Head of Brân on the wooden steps.

And I caught it!

I caught it, and turned it to the south-east and braced myself as I crouched down jamming the Head under my chin as Sian Llewelyn fell to her knees, screaming and crawling into the White Tower like some feathered monster under a mass of jabbering, jabbing birds.

And at the bottom of the stairs I could see James. He started climbing the steps towards me.

'No, no, no,' he was muttering to himself, his hair dark flopping into his lovely face. 'Can't have an injured leader, can't let that happen. Oh, no.'

Hugging himself, he hurried up the steps towards me in his camouflage jacket, and I knew at that moment why it was baggy. I knew that inside it was a bomb.

His blue eyes seemed to look right through me as he passed.

'James!' I said to him, panicking.

'Boom!' he grinned, and his lovely face looked entirely happy. 'See you in the Otherworld, Ava!' and he went into the White Tower and dived on Sian in a rugby tackle. The birds fluttered and screeched, and the words SUCCESFUL ENTERPRISE screamed in my brain and I jumped fifteen feet from the wooden steps, pressing my face against the skull as the world exploded in a cloud of heat and smoke and pain.

I didn't hear the bang.

Chapter Twenty-Seven

I didn't hear anything clearly for quite a while.

I choked on the black smoke and the heat of the flames and then I was arrested by the Yeoman Warders.

In the days that followed, Tal, Rosie and I had to go through 'debriefings' in the Tower barracks.

We got asked a lot of questions and I tried to tell them the truth. The fact is, I was too scared not to. I told them everything, about Idrys and his lost memories and the image in Nain's glasses. They listened to my answers, but like my dad, they decided not to believe it. I don't blame them. If it hadn't happened to me personally I wouldn't either.

They wanted to know how we knew about the Head when it was a secret that even people who worked there didn't know about. They wanted to know about the 'major bird strike' as they called it, and how Tal had controlled it.

They asked about Gwilliam and when we said he was going to steal the Head for money they charged him with 'conspiracy to cause a public nuisance'. He's not going to be a rich hippy in Goa. Not for the moment, anyway.

They wanted to know why James had run inside the White Tower where the thickness of the stone walls contained the blast, preventing many deaths. And they asked us why James had killed himself and Sian, seeing as she was his one and only friend.

I was going to explain that you had to kill an injured leader when Tal interrupted me.

'He dreamed of being a druid,' he told them softly. 'But his mind didn't work the right way for that. He had a lonely life. He liked destroying things too much.'

Tal changed, that day in the Tower, in more ways than one. He found his confidence and discovered his druidic powers. Idrys would be proud of him.

In the days that followed he reasoned with the Yeomen Warders that now the secret of the Head was out, it wasn't fair that Brân wasn't getting any credit for protecting the country when he was doing such a good job of it.

So two things have happened. They have now mentioned Brân the Blessed on the information by the ravens' enclosure, and they have secured the Head in the chapel with a 'top spec. security system' in case anyone else has the bright idea of moving it from the place it belongs.

I feel different, too.

I surprised (and impressed) a lot of people because of my swim into the Tower through the wells. I'm the only person that's ever done it in the history of the Tower. No-one even knew that it was possible, and it's lucky I didn't know that beforehand because I would never have tried it.

And in case anyone wants to try this for themselves, I wouldn't, if I were you. Firstly, take it from me, your Dad will freak out. Secondly, there is now a Perspex cover over the well in the White Tower gift shop. You'd never get out.

And this is what *didn't* happen.

My mum didn't come home.

The Head, those holy bones as good as a platinum credit card at making dreams come true had given me two things that I wanted. It had brought Tal back to life and it had made Nain better again.

I wished that in those moments before the guards arrested me, when the world was on fire and that BOOM blasted my ears with a sound so loud that it was like being punched by the fist of God that I could have held it against my chest for five minutes longer and asked for one last thing.

'We did it,' Tal said to me this morning, tossing his black t-shirts into a bag, in other words, packing. 'We went a funny way about it, but we protected the Head, just as Idrys told us to. You know something, Ava? It's the safest that Head's ever been since it was cut off.'

I hadn't thought of it like that, and it made me smile.

We drove him and Nain to Euston Station and waved them off. We felt pretty sad, saying goodbye. Caroline offered me her waterproof mascara and Dad sniffed a lot and said he had an allergy coming on.

I can still feel Nain's gentle hug and Tal's thump on my arm. I miss him already. So that's why I'm writing everything down. I'm writing it down to remember it. And the great thing is, if I need to check anything, I can always ask him.

I've learnt something this summer. For a start, that it's good to be argumentative for the right reasons. Don't let people tell you it's not! See – that's an argument for you right there. You can't go along with things just because people tell you to, or because you don't think you have the power to make things right. We all have power. We have more than we ever think.

'Ava?' Dad yelled.

'What?'

'Come here a minute.'

'But I'm writing-' I've got arm-ache and in any case I've come to the end of the story, so I put my pen down and go into the kitchen to see what he wants.

He's sitting at the table looking awkward and his red hair is sticking up madly. 'This business with Gwilliam and Sian Llewelyn... I don't know how you did it.' He scratches his head and turns pink. 'We've got two weeks of the

270

holidays left.' He slaps a printed boarding pass on the table. 'We're going to see Mum in Nepal.'

I hug him so hard that he struggles for air.

'One thing I've learnt out of all this, Ava,' he gasps. 'You can never judge a book by its cover.'

Author's Notes

I've had great fun writing about Ava, Tal and the legend of Brân's Head, and I hope you've had fun too. If you've got any questions about the story or you want to know what happens next, get in touch!

Thank you, Elaine Cauthery, for being the first to read the Ava Jones story and Trisha Ashley for judging it with your writer's eyes – you powered me on!

Sarah Deco and Mary Ann Kurtz have been in on this story from the beginning – that's ten good years of fun, friendship and literary talk.

Bridget Whelan has shared her abundance of creative enthusiasm and Edward Milner, film maker, literary critic and bibliophile, produced the video – here's to the City Lit Three.

Rowena has passed on her love of Welsh literature. See? I was listening!

A large part of writing is taken up with avoiding it and the winners of the distraction category are Mary de Laszlo, Margaret James, Jane Tilbrook, Sarah House and Tina Mahoney.

I'd like to thank my Godchildren William, Callum, Charlotte, Ellie and Harry for all-round loveliness; Chloe, for the pictures of Ava, Ella for styling and Tallulah for her review

and

With warmest greetings to the readers at Killigrew Primary School, who love books and storytelling.

www.normacurtis.com

6913492R00155

Printed in Great Britain
by Amazon.co.uk, Ltd.,
Marston Gate.